It al

Om sis of everything prized in his pack something eminded him of often as a child when his skinny physique and academic goals kept him on the outside looking in. Leaving his pack to attend university while most of the pups are just beginning high school has given him the freedom to explore all the academics he's always longed to, but something is missing. Even years later when he finds his roommate and they form their own makeshift pack, he still feels off-center, like there's a hole in his life.

And then he's invited to the shifter hotspot Animals for their annual Halloween party. This will change everything. He can feel it. He just has no idea how much.

It all started with a job offer...

Alpha Bruin spends his life traveling across the country installing eco-friendly updates to businesses. It's a rewarding job, but a very lonely life. Not that he has anything to go back to. When his brother took over as clan leader, Bruin was given an ultimatum. He could challenge his brother or accept exile. Knowing a challenge would lead to his brother's death, he chose never to return again. The sacrifice has been worth it. Mostly.

His latest work project, the club Animals, turns out to feel more like home than anyplace he's been since his clan. When the project ends, he isn't ready yet to leave, willingly accepting an invitation to their Halloween shindig.

When Darius and Bruin meet it's lust at first sight. Darius brings out the daddy in Bruin who helps him discover a side of himself he never suspected he had. If only it wasn't Bruin's last day at Animals...in the country, for that matter.

Copyright

Papa Bear for Darius

ISBN: 978-1-68361-356-5

Print ISBN: 978-1-68361-573-6

Cover design by Fantasia Frog Designs

Published by Decadent Publishing LLC

Papa Bear for Darius
Omegas of Animals

By

Lorelei M. Hart

Prologue

Darius

"It's going to be a night to remember, that's for sure." Cal, an alpha lion shifter if my nose was accurate, which it tended to be, had officially taken over the chemistry study group I had decided to test the waters by joining. Not that I needed such a group to help me pass the class. I could easily teach the course, but it was lonely wearing my shoes, and I wanted to create a place I could shine and possibly finally meet some friends.

I'd misunderstood what a study group was. So far, they had discussed three "hawt" professors, who, to be fair, were nice looking, and two upcoming frat parties. Just when I thought we'd moved on to a topic I could contribute to in a less than awkward manner, they started on about Animals, a shifter nightclub out in the desert a fair drive from campus, but a drive they all swore was worth it. The last part caught my attention if for no other reason than the guy I had dreams about getting naked with had been talking about it earlier when I wasn't eavesdropping...much.

"I'm hitting it up. Halloween parties are my jam." A female alpha punched the arm of the guy to the left of her. I couldn't figure out what exactly she was trying to accomplish with that move, possibly some kind of mating ritual, but all it got her was a growl—and not the sexy kind I had read about in books. It still cafuddled me how I could already have multiple college degrees and still not be able to understand the people around me, the ones who were finally just about peer level—at least age wise.

When I entered college at fifteen, I thought I would take on the world. I didn't have the clan hierarchy holding me back as I had at home. I thought my fellow students would be mostly humans, and easier to deal with because they didn't have hierarchies. I'd been so incredibly naive. True, there were more humans than shifters, by a significant percentage, and, no, there weren't clan dynamics. Where I'd completely gotten it wrong was in my assumption I could somehow navigate this world and fit in. Even at eighteen, I'd not yet found my niche.

I would though. It was just going to take time. As my late mama used to say when I was growing up, the rest of the world just needed to catch up to me. She had referred to the other pups, but I held on to her promise like a lifeline.

"I can snag a van." A third person, one everyone had ignored the entire night even when he tried to interject his opinions on the subject at hand, finally gained the floor. "I mean, my dad lets me take it sometimes. I just need to have it back at the store when they open in the morning, and we can all chip in to fill the tank before we return it."

"And you, Joshua, are my favorite person." The alpha leaned back, a victorious grin across his face.

"The party starts at seven. Who's in?" Matt, the fox who had originally announced the study group, asked. He was also the only one besides me who showed any inclination of wanting to actually break open some notes or a book. But with the party, a theme night at that, less of a hypothetical and more of a reality, he was all in on the not studying plan.

And that was when I made the decision that ultimately changed my life. "I have a gas card." Awkward as fuck, but given Joshua's currency had been the van, gas money seemed a logical offering. "So we all have more money for the club."

And I was going to Animals for the first time. I was under no delusion the group had accepted me or I'd run into my crush and we'd live happily ever after.

I'd kind of figured out over my time at the university that I might never fit in, not really. Heck, if you can't fit in with your own pack, that was pretty much an indication of how your life away would go as well. I just wished I'd learned the lesson years earlier. It would've made me happier. Not that I fully learned it, as obvious by the attendance at the study group.

***

"The line is long today." Cal acted as if he was a regular. Given he hadn't known where to park, I fought to not roll my eyes.

Shifters. So many shifters. Not what struck me as odd. It was Animals, after all. What struck me as peculiar was how many humans were interspersed among them and how they appeared to know the score—that the majority of people milling around with them could take their fur at any second.

I was awed. And as we slowly inched forward, I found myself listening to those around us, ignoring the small group I'd come with. They only let me come because of my stupid gas card, the one I'd picked up on my way back to my crappy apartment. It had gotten me here now, and, as I listened to the bears and lions and wolves and even a koala, somehow, I just knew this was where I was meant to be.

The bouncer at the door disagreed. Told me to come back when I was legal. And as was the way of true friends, the group I came with cracked up as they walked in, leaving me stranded. I couldn't be mad. My not even thinking about the fact bars require you to be legal only showed me face on how desperate I'd been.

Worst part was, I probably would do it again. My brain had a way of forgetting the important things when it came to social situations, and I found myself messing up—a lot. Like the time I thought I could pledge to a frat house at sixteen, or the time I asked my former professor to dinner, not realizing she thought I was asking her on a date and not trying to make a friend. I assured her I wasn't looking for a female, falling back into shifter speak. I still couldn't look her in the eye two years later.

Social and I were not on the best of terms.

"You." A woman's voice startled me. She was close, close enough I should have heard her coming—and I would have had I not been so into my head. Which wasn't the safest way to be as I leaned against Joshua's father's van, waiting for who knew how long for them to get done with their fun.

“Me?”

“You are the one who came with those selfish pups?” Her hands were her hips, and I couldn’t tell if it was because she was posturing or because she was showing off her themed outfit, complete with glitter...so much glitter.

“Probably,” I conceded.

“You don’t belong here yet.” Her turn of phrase felt so purposeful.

“Yet?” I blurted before I could think better of it.

“Yes. Your invitation will come.” She waved, and a headlight shone in my direction. “Now, off with you.” The headlight turned out to be on a little beater of a car with a rideshare logo in the window. “He will take you home. No, not home, but back to your place. You’ll know when it’s time to come back.” She tapped her lip, nodded at the hired car, and turned on her toe, walking away and into the arms of a man I hadn’t noticed there. So weird.

Not being able to think of anything else to do, I climbed into the car and calculated my funds in my head. If the driver could get me to the edge of town, I could catch a bus. Buying the gas card had not been my best idea. Or maybe it was. I still couldn’t decipher the conversation with the weird woman.

"Can you just drop me off at the first bus stop?" I took out my wallet and counted my cash. Not much. Not much at all.

"You're not going to the east side?" He turned around. The guy had to be close to my age, and his scent was familiar...but not.

"You take a class in Science Building 3, ending at 2:50 on Mondays and Wednesdays." I finally placed his scent from when I walked into my three o'clock class, and blurted the information out before considering how creepy I sounded. "I'm not a stalker."

"No, I suppose not." He chuckled. "I'm Basil, and welcome to my side hustle, at least until this thing fails inspection next month. The fare is paid to the east side, so I need to go there anyway to get paid. GPS, you know."

"I'm Darius. Paid?"

"Indeed. So what do you say?"

"East side, please." I leaned back, feeling more at ease with this stranger than I had with anyone in a long time. By the time we pulled up to my building, I'd made a friend and, by month's end, got my first roommate. That evening had been a catalyst for so many wonderful changes in my life. It took years before I discovered them all.

Chapter One

Bruin

Three years later...

I lifted the "dad hat" from my head and ruffled my hair. When Karma invited me to stay for the Halloween party before catching my flight to Spain for my next project, I'd agreed before knowing costumes were required. When I tried to gracefully back out on that basis, she waved away my concerns by offering to provide something for me to wear.

When I protested again, Warren growled. The bear owner of Animals was my third cousin on my mother's side, and had an almost "godfather" standing. He was very protective of his mate's feelings, and because offending a client/relative/really huge bear was a bad idea, I had agreed to attend the Animals Annual Halloween Bash as Papa Bear. How she'd found a suit in my size, I'd never know.

I'd been here working on eco-friendly updates for a couple of weeks, but, in truth, it was the easiest job I'd ever taken on. I'd already done Crossroads, the sister club in New Orleans, which had been a bit more of a challenge because they'd set up in a historical French Quarter building and were dealing with a century-and-a-half-old structure for which they couldn't make many external changes. But Animals, set as it was in front of an ancient shifter cliff dwelling, had been built from the ground up with modern Earth-friendly materials and systems. Still, new technology came along every year, and Warren and Karma were very interested in walking lightly, especially since the lights and music of their type of business used a great deal of energy by its nature. Their carbon footprint was now less than the average residential home. I was good at my job.

The club was decorated to within an inch of its life. And it did seem to have its own life. The feel of the cliff dwelling lingered, the many shifters who'd lived and died blessing the location. I had wondered briefly what the ancestors would think of the welcoming of not only every other paranormal but even humans...but times changed.

And the clan I grew up in would not have welcomed other shifters, much less witches, trolls, ogres, and the fae—all of whom were here dancing, drinking, gobbling food at the buffet—and certainly not ordinary humans. I liked this system better. Once in a while, I missed my brother or cousins on my dad's side of the family, none of whom would welcome me after the way I left, but spending time with Warren and Karma and their staff had been more than pleasant. At their invitation, I would return for a visit as soon as my schedule allowed.

As I moved through the crowd, though, I remembered why I avoided parties. People were laughing together and dancing. Lots of hugging and kissing and, in the booths along the walls, some of the more graphic PDA that happened at shifter clubs. We were not hung up on nudity or public sex—at least some of us—a reason most facilities didn't let others in. We liked to be ourselves.

"Bruin!" Karma appeared from the doorway to the office hallway. "Have you found him yet?"

"Sorry?" Was I supposed to be looking for Warren or something? "Can't you find your mate?"

"Not him. I always know where he is." She linked her arm with mine and led me toward the entrance.

"How do you do that? Are you sure you're a garden variety human?" Some might take offense but not Cousin Karma.

Her laughter peeled out. "You're so silly. Don't most couples of all kinds have a bond or a link? They even start to look like each other after a while, they say."

I dug in my heels and looked at her. She was pretty and curvy and wore enough sparkles to light up a small city. Her hair was in an elaborate updo contained in a net woven with more crystals or something shiny. "Karma, I don't think you look anything like your mate."

She winked, long lashes sweeping her cheek. "And thank goodness. But one more trip past the buffet might change that. Have you tried the hot pepper mummies? Oh my gosh."

"No, I haven't had anything to eat yet. Maybe I should go do that now." Eating would take up some time, and then I could have a drink or two and slip away back to the guest suite behind the club in the cliff dwelling. How they'd managed to make use of the rooms while maintaining their historical integrity was a thing of wonder. I tried to head across the room toward the food, but Karma gripped my arm tighter.

"Oh no you don't." She craned her neck to see around a pair of giraffes dressed as ghosts just entering. "You have to be right here when he comes. It's important."

"Who are we talking about? Is there someone you

need me to keep an eye on?" Because truly, once you let all this variety of folks in, you were taking a chance on someone annoying someone else.

"No, no!" Her annoyed tone didn't make sense. "I have plenty of employees. You're here to have fun."

"Then who do you want me to meet?" She was being decidedly obtuse. Then it occurred to me. "Is it someone else who does eco work?" With so few of us in the paranormal world, visiting with someone who shared my passion was always a treat. "Maybe an environmental disposal specialist? Someone in solar?"

She giggled again. "Is it all about work with you, Papa Bear? I said fun."

One of the servers came up and leaned in to speak close to her ear, and she sighed. "Well, heck. I thought I could be here to see, but I have a small emergency in the kitchen."

"Emergency?"

"Kind of a fire."

I reeled back. "A fire? Has anyone called the fire department?"

She snorted. "Out here? Nobody official knows we're here."

"With a crowd like this?" I waved around. "How?"

"Oh, ask Warren. I don't deal with that stuff. But I

do need to go make sure the fire is out and nobody got hurt." She released me and took a step away.

"I'll come with you—"

"No!"

I jerked back at her vehemence. "Why not?"

She came close again and held my gaze, speaking in a low, serious tone. "You need to be right here when he comes. These things...timing is critical. Now, promise me you'll stay here until you meet him."

I was starting to wonder if planning this event had been too much for Karma, but upsetting her would only piss off Warren, and arguing would keep her from dealing with a serious situation. "I promise. I will."

A smile lit her face. "Perfect. I'll check in on you later, but you won't need me. I'm so excited." Then she turned and headed toward the kitchen, the crowd melting away from her stiletto-heeled strides. Even if she was a little strange tonight, my cousin had met his perfect mate. They loved each other fiercely and unconditionally, and it was hard not to be jealous. I leaned against the wall and watched the crowd pour into the building, filling every space. No wonder they wouldn't want the fire department here. They'd force half of these people out again. At least this was a good place to people watch.

One fellow was knocked askew and landed in another's arms... What a way to meet.

Chapter Two

Darius

"Basil, quit being stubborn." I loosened my grip on my invitation. *The invitation.* The one I had been waiting for since that night years ago. No way was I not going—but that didn't mean I was ready to wander in there on my own, either. Especially not when the invitation stated specifically it was for me and a friend—not a date, a friend.

When I met Karma that night in the parking lot, she scented human, but not. At the time, I didn't think much of it, my entire evening having gone so horribly wrong I'd been in a pity party for one until I met my future bestie and roommate. And then Monday came and ,with it, a letter from my uncle Paul, and the pieces fell into place. Some part, and I wasn't sure what size part, of Karma was *other* and, if I were to wager, that *other* held the ability to see. And it was with that lens her word choices felt beyond intentional. So if she said friend, Basil, being the sole owner of the title, was coming with me.

"This was hand delivered. Hand. Delivered." I

waved the glitter-filled card in his face. I didn't know if I was coming off as desperate or crazy, and, truly, I didn't care. The compulsion for me to bring him with me superseded all else. "Do you know how long I have waited for this?"

He, of course, did. If it weren't for him, I'd have been in the Animals parking lot all night, waiting for my so-called friends' sorry asses. The study group didn't have the decency to apologize or pretend to care what happened to me that night when I saw them in class the next time.

I watched as his eyes showed signs of him beginning to cave.

"Since you first heard about it?"

"No." I plopped down beside him on the couch, still clutching the invitation I'd somehow been granted for their Halloween party. "The first time I heard about the club was from Prof. Jones, and it was in a conversation I wished I'd never walked into." It had never been easy being so young on campus, but morphing from a boy to a man then had led to more than a few awkward moments.

"That's... I have no words." He shivered, and I watched him, unsure what to say. He must've noticed, adding on, "So, how long?"

"Remember Lionel?" He nodded as I brought up my first big crush. "He was sitting at the table next to mine at the school coffee shop the day before my eighteenth birthday and told his friend he was going to Animals that weekend."

Basil's head dropped. The day changed my life—or more accurately, his side hustle had.

"I tried to get in by tagging along with my study group, but the bouncer said I wasn't old enough, and the woman who ordered my ride, Karma, pulled me aside and said she'd send me an invite when it was time." Basil knew all this, but it was all I had left. Playing on his emotions could no way be construed as the nicest way to get what I wanted. I kind of stank.

I'd never told him about Karma. It somehow felt too personal and, given his quizzical expression, offering him more details wouldn't have been the worst of ideas. And then I remembered the four bazillion human events he'd dragged me to, since he didn't like to be in predominantly shifter groups. He said it was because his latency made the others feel uncomfortable, but I knew better. He was uncomfortable. He never saw the amazing shifter he was, allowing his lack of fur to shape his self-worth.

I was one to talk. I let my pack's disapproval of all

I was do the same to me. Probably why we were such good friends.

"Fine. I'll go, but only because I owe you, and I am not wearing a costume."

Oh, he was so wearing a costume.

***

"You could have been so much cuter as 'Little Red' if you had let me dress you." I grabbed his arm and tugged him the half step we'd managed to move in the past half hour—and I still couldn't see the club door. Every shifter on the planet must've gotten an invitation to this party. It was going to be amazing.

The scents around me ranged from nervous to excited to horny. I couldn't wait.

"I don't want to hear it."

I'd found him so many costumes, ranging from cute to sexy, and what did he go with? He went with a hoodie—a stupid red hoodie.

"I'd catch my death of cold." His exaggerated tone and hand gestures had a shifter a few feet in front of us attempting, very poorly, to control his laughter.

"I wasn't even thinking the jock one," I lied. I totally was. Basil needed to get laid or blown or something, and his outfit was perfection.

"Your nose is growing."

I reached for my nose and caught Basil's eyeroll and wanted to join him. Leave it to me to take him so literally. Not the first time I'd misread a social cue or two, and it certainly wouldn't be the last.

"You—in the hood and ears," barked a big guy I could only assume was a bouncer given his all-black ensemble, bulging muscles, and a hat emblazoned with *Animals*.

"Me?" I squeaked, and I grabbed my bunny ears from my head. Why had I worn such a submissive outfit to a party filled with shifters? *Because you want to submit*. There was that. I pointed to myself as I stared at the bouncer's hat.

"Yeah, you, EB. You got an invite, right?"

Perking up, I reached into my pocket and yanked out the now rumpled mess of an invitation, trying to figure out why he'd called me EB but too afraid to ask for fear my invitation would somehow be invalidated.

"Yes...sir." I held it out as the man walked away. Didn't he want to see it? I'd want to see it.

"Coming or not? We are almost at capacity," he yelled, and I scurried to catch up to him as the EB comment fell into place. Easter Bunny. I had been going for sexy submissive, but there were worse names than EB.

We headed straight for the front of the line. A man wearing the same outfit as the bouncer—with the exception of a small *Candy Security* logo on the left side of his chest—held the door for us. "You just made it. Lucky Karma intervened."

I'd expected greatness. I'd be lying if I said anything else, but the place far exceeded my wildest imagination. Everything from the band to the lights to the non-security staff shouted Halloween. There was even orange-and-black beer somehow layered in the mugs in stripes—which ewwwww—yet cool. And everyone, at least everyone but my roomie, bought into the theme, decked out in their Halloween best. So worth the wait.

"Darius." Karma stepped in close, and it was all I could do not to wrap my arms around her, to thank her for remembering me and sending the key to the most exciting night of my life so far. "I'm so glad you and your friend accepted my invitation. I have some things I want to show you." She took my arm then gave Basil a wink. "We'll be back. You just have fun."

She led me a short distance to the end of a bar; they had at least six I'd already seen. The place was mammoth. Karma pointed to an empty seat next to a man dressed in a toga. “Sit here, Darius. I need to take care of something.” She scratched the tip of her nose then looked back and forth at something I couldn’t determine. “There may be some issue I need to handle first.” And she was gone.

I took the seat and grabbed the napkin in front of me, more for something to do than anything else. Questions—so many questions bounced around in my head. Why did she want to see me? What did she mean about having fun? What issue? The last one wasn’t my business, but once my brain got on a roll, it just kept going.

“Whatcha drinking?” the bartender asked. It wasn’t a challenging question, not by anyone’s standards, yet, for a few seconds, the answer evaded me.

“Ummm, cola?” I finally spit out, knowing I didn’t want to drink alcohol and ordering water was not the way to keep my seat unless I wanted to fill a landfill with a plastic bottle. Alcohol sounded like a good way to make a potentially great night go instantly south. With holding it together in social situations rough for me on a good day, adding alcohol to the mix was self-sabotage technique number one. The bartender nodded and moved away.

"I got the same response over my milk." I turned to the guy in the toga. Point proven. How long had I been sitting by him and not once acknowledged his existence.

"Probably thinks I won't tip well, but I will. I just think maybe I shouldn't drink until I get my bearings on this place. I can't believe I'm here. I've been wanting to come for so long." I continued to play with my napkin.

"I never heard of this place until today." He took a long sip of his milk.

I could definitely see how a bartender would find that odd. Who drank milk? Children and pregnant—ohhhh—how had I missed a pregnancy? It wasn't like his toga hid anything. It did the opposite. I needed to pay more attention.

"They sure go all-out on the festivities, don't they?" He pointed to the pumpkin-light-mirror ball over the dance area, and his scent filled my nose. It was different-ish. Maybe it was the pregnancy. I'd scented him coming in only not.

"Huh." I leaned in closer and then not so subtly sniffed him. I knew better. That was how I'd ended up with my first broken bone in middle school—Johnny scented different, and I leaned in close enough to get his fist in my face. If they had told us puberty scented differently, I wouldn't have gotten into so much trouble, but then again, I was eight and didn't belong there in the first place, not anyway but academically anyway. "Your scent...I usually remember a scent accurately, but I could've sworn you were more allspice than nutmeg. Huh."

I'd only noticed and remembered because of the allspice. It had always been a favorite of mine, even if most of my clan denied there was a discernible difference between allspice and nutmeg. They were wrong. So wrong.

His face fell, or was it excitement? I couldn't tell, but my words impacted him deeply.

"Where did you scent me?" He more stammered than spoke. "The first time." He clarified.

"In line. You probably didn't see me. They pulled me out of line, and I walked past you. I don't remember the toga, but I was more focused on getting in." I shrugged as he slid off his chair.

"Nice to meet you. I gotta go." He waddled toward I didn't know where. If this was how my night was going to go, maybe I'd set my expectations a bit too high.

Chapter Three

Bruin

After a minute or two, the tumbling omega was caught by Chris, an alpha and a bartender who was attending the event as a guest at the insistence of the bosses. Where most businesses I did work for had a tough time attracting quality staff, and shifters were notorious for having lax work habits anyway, the people at Animals seemed dedicated to the point they had to be forced to take time off.

I could understand. They were treated more as family than workers, paid well, and some lived on-site in the super-amazing cliff dwelling. I'd seen one job open up, in maintenance, while I was here. The janitor in question was called home to help care for his sick alpha dad, but he'd be back as soon as his father either passed or recovered. I'd heard him assuring Warren of that and asking his job be held. Only a temp had been hired.

Chris and the omega melted into the crowd, and I noted with amusement our wolf bartender had found himself a guy in a red hoodie—fairy tale in progress?

At least maybe they'd have a fun night. He needed one.

But then, so did I. People still flowed in, though I couldn't imagine where they'd go. Soon, the dance floor would be a standing room only floor. But Animals had an amazing ability to hold more guests than it seemed as if it could. Part of the magic of the place.

How long was I supposed to stand here and wait for whoever or whatever Karma wanted me to see? Maybe I could zip over to the bar, get a drink, and return. But as I considered my options, someone stepped on my food, hard.

"Hey!" I yanked my foot back with a growl. "What the hell, buddy?" It didn't hurt much, but it was damn startling.

The tiger dressed as a lion—nothing weird there—growled at me and stomped off, managing to hit my other foot on the way, but I didn't follow to knock his lights out. Not because I didn't want to and not because that would be a poor way to repay hospitality. My bear didn't have manners of that level. No...my bear was focused on Karma heading my way with an omega bunny on her arm. No...not a bunny. A bear dressed as a bunny.

What was with all the animals being other animals around here? Didn't he like his bear side? Still, something about the little bear with the big glasses tore right into my gut. My bear was dancing and growling and having a bear fiesta in there, which is less comfortable than you might think. *Mate. Mate. Mate.*

Oh, hell no. Sure, he was cute, and as he nodded vigorously to something Karma said to him, his ears slid down to join his glasses on the tip of his nose. He readjusted them with his free hand. My mouth went dry, my hands were sweating, and everything suave about me went out the window as they arrived in front of me and said, "Here he is. Darius, this is Bruin. Bruin, Darius." She freed her arm and gave him a little push toward me. "You two be good now...don't do anything my mate and I wouldn't do. Not without video." Her laughter trailed behind her as she disappeared into the crowd, the last sight of her a wink of the pumpkin disco ball light on the sparkles in her hair.

And there we stood looking at each other, the wild music of the band led by the redheaded devil filling all the air around us. Finally, I nodded. "Nice to meet you, Darius. Want to get a drink?"

"Yes!" His enthusiasm was startling. "I mean, sure that would be nice."

"This way." I cupped his elbow and guided him

out a side door onto the cliff where a flat open space allowed a view of the desert floor below.

He dug in his heels and looked panicked for a moment. “I thought we were going to the bar?” The moonlight reflected off his glasses, enhancing a smudge in one corner. Too adorable for words.

So I kissed him. Released his elbow, wrapped an arm around him, and bent to press my lips against his without waiting for permission or possible refusal. I blame my bear. But Darius didn’t’ refuse or try to get away. He tipped his head back and parted his lips to admit my questing tongue. Our teeth clicked together, but neither of us complained. He tasted like Dr. Pepper, which he had probably been drinking on the way here, but under that lay a different sweetness I couldn’t get enough of. Perfection. I lapped at every inch of his mouth, exploring and returning to catch his tongue with mine and entwine them.

I wasn’t sure if the groan was mine or his, but it didn’t matter. We were already fumbling at our clothes while I backed him toward the cliff face, kissing the whole time. If I didn’t get his costume off in two seconds, I was going to shred it off and be damned the consequences. Be damned everything.

I left his lips behind to follow my fingers as they

revealed his skin by inches, kissing the hollow of his throat, nibbling his collarbone, swirling my tongue around a flat, masculine nipple. Everything about him aroused me, including the little pants and whines he emitted when I bit down on that nipple.

I was about ready to drop to my knees and suck him dry when laughter came from behind me and I froze. Sure, shifters were willing to have sex in public. I might—admitting to nothing—have done so myself, once upon a time. But not with my mate.

Shut up, no he's not.

Mate!

I pulled Darius tight against me as the group of whispering, giggling swan shifters passed us then strolled to the edge of the cliff to look out over the desert. They peeked over their shoulders and laughed some more, showing no signs of leaving anytime soon.

Finally, I took a step back and adjusted both of our clothing. "Let's get that drink."

His head bobbed, but a glance downward showed his cock was as hard and ready as mine, albeit in a silly rabbit suit. "Okay. I want a carrot juice and vodka."

I chuckled but then realized he was serious. "Oh, sure. We'll see if the bar has any carrot juice." There were some regular rabbit shifters here. They probably ordered it. We started toward the door, but I stopped him just outside and ground my lips on his. “Let’s go to the party. But afterward, I’d like to invite you to my place for... Well, I don’t have any carrot juice, but maybe coffee?”

His tongue came out and moistened his swollen lips. I groaned deep inside. Probably had been me before. “Papa, let’s not dance too long.”

Chapter Four

Darius

My cola arrived, and I gave the bartender a five dollar bill, telling him to keep the change, which, for all I knew, was two cents. Places this popular could charge whatever they wanted, and people would pay—at least I would. He smiled and thanked me, so I took it as a sign I didn't blow it and rotated around, cup in hand, to people watch.

A good chunk of me wanted to follow the pregnant omega and figure out what had set him off about our conversation—besides me getting all awkward and such. I also wanted to check on Basil. He didn't want to be here, and, given the intensity of the party, my guilt at dragging him along was starting to settle in. I'd promised Karma I'd stay, though, so I fought the impulse to do otherwise and sipped on my cola, which had turned out to be Dr. Pepper, as the band started yet another of their tribute songs. They sounded at least as good as the original band, possibly better.

And then there was a shift in the air. It was so subtle and so many of the shifters so well on their way to being dressed in liquor it was most likely missed by three quarters or more of the room. It was palpable, though—like the change in the taste of the air just before a clan challenge or as an Alpha steps down.

Except this place had nothing to do with packs or alphas, not in that sense, anyway. It was a club celebrating a festive night. I darted my tongue out, attempting to taste the air. It rarely worked, but sometimes it did, so it was worth the try. It tasted different, somehow, but not discernable enough for me. I exhaled as much as I could and sucked in a huge breath through my nose.

Anger.

There was anger somewhere, anger enough to cause violence. I looked for the nearest exit as a few security guards wove through the crowd and, suddenly, just like that, it was gone. I chose to believe it was because they managed to quell whatever was escalating. Shifters had tempers, some animals more than others. It just was the way it was.

I took another sip of my soda. My hands were already starting to get jittery from the caffeine and sugar. I'd have been better off copying the omega who'd been beside me and ordering milk.

I placed it on the counter and pulled out my cell

phone to see if Basil was searching for me.

"No phones," a bouncer walking past scolded.

"Sorry." I mumbled, sliding it back into my pocket. I didn't know it was a rule. Or maybe it wasn't, and he was thinking I was doing something wrong. I didn't even know.

"You ready?" Karma startled me. How a human in shoes so tall could sneak up on anyone was beyond me, yet there she was doing exactly that.

"Sure?" I slid off my seat. "May I ask for what?" When I'd gotten the invitation, I'd thought it simply meant I could get in this time, very much unlike the last time. Wrong.

"You may." She cut through the crowds, and it took four steps for me to realize she'd out played me using my own words. When we stopped, I would ask her exactly what I was to be ready for, not if I could ask her. Duh.

The costumed partygoers almost looked like they were choreographed to sway out of her way as she walked. Me? Not so much. It took me at least double the effort to keep up with her. And yet, I couldn't be mad about it. There was just something about her.

She finally stopped, and, at first, I assumed it was to allow me to catch up, but then she began introductions. And then it hit me. The scent. His scent. The scent made for me, the one telling me, without a single doubt, the man connected to it was my mate. I peered around to see who owned the blend of frankincense and lavender.

"Here he is." She patted my shoulder, and my eyes followed hers.

The fates were smiling down on me. The older alpha, complete with Papa Bear hat and a tailored suit, checked every single box I had for physical preferences: hot. Yeah, I wasn't overly specific in my desires for what my mate looked like. I just wished more than once I'd be one of the lucky few who found their true fated mates, and since I had, I kicked myself for wasting time on crushes and half-ass attempts at finding a boyfriend. Everything came down to this man—this alpha. And the crazy thing was, I didn't know his name.

"Darius, this is Bruin. Bruin, Darius." She freed her arm and gave me a little push toward the man in front of me. Not that I needed one. I could barely hear his name over my dumb-ass animal's insistence on yelling at me he was our mate.

"You two be good now...don't do anything my mate and I wouldn't do. Not without video."

Video? Gulp.

And on that note, she danced away, although it wasn't technically dancing, but her gracefulness gave it all the same attributes.

Was that what this entire thing was? Karma's way of giving me my fated mate or vice versa or whatever? It sounded farfetched, and yet that was exactly what she'd done. Maybe her other-ness was fae. They had so many abilities far surpassing ours as shifters.

"Nice to meet you, Darius. Want to get a drink?"

"Yes!" I snapped my mouth shut at my zeal. Zeal at something I didn't want. I wasn't planning on drinking. I wanted to remember every single second of tonight. "I mean, sure, it would be nice." My attempt at correction amused him enough he gave me a grin, one having me willing to beg for a nibble of those lips.

"This way." He led me not to the bar, but to the dance floor. I was confused to say the least.

"I thought we were going to the bar?" He didn't answer me with words. Instead, he leaned in and kissed me. No, that wasn't right. He didn't kiss me, he possessed my lips, and by the time our lips broke apart, my knees weak and my body breathless, all I wanted to do was ask him to be my Papa.

And I might have, too, if he didn't yank me to his

body to get me out of the way of some annoying kids—kids who were probably my exact age. So, adults?

He took a step back after they were past, and I gave a quick peek around the area, and when deeming it good enough, pulled on my pants enough to give my cock breathing room. Darn thing had been hard as a rock at first scent, and I had a feeling nothing but his knot would remedy the situation.

"Let's get that drink."

"Okay. I want a carrot juice and vodka."

He chuckled, and, for half a second, I wondered if he thought it was my bad attempt at a joke. It hadn't been, but it had been a bad idea. Carrot juice was fine—one of my favorites from the year my mom accidentally grew enough carrots for the universe, thinking she was planting baby carrots. I still teased her about how she ruined me, turning me into a rabbit. Fair to say I hadn't thought out my costume as much as might've been prudent.

"Oh, sure. We'll see if the bar has any carrot juice."

I didn't know if he read my expression or just changed his mind, but instead of going to the bar, I found him kissing me once more. So much better than a drink.

"Let's go to the party. But afterward, I'd like to

invite you back to my place for... Well, I don't have any carrot juice, but maybe coffee?"

"Papa, let's not dance too long." And...I changed everything. I hadn't meant for it to come out all lusty and sex. I'd simply read his hat, and yet, once the words passed through my lips, they took on their own life. Papa. Submission had been in my blood...I'd always at least suspected that, but to feel it so tangibly with a simple word was the epitome of what meeting a true mate was, wasn't it? He was my Papa—my papa. My bear begged to bare my neck. My cock begged, standing harder than should be physically possible. My hole begged for him.

One word was all it took.

And it wasn't one-sided. No, not even close. His eyes darkened in an instant as the word escaped my lips.

"Do you need a papa?" *Heck yeah I did.* His lips brushed my ear, and a shiver ran through me. If a brush of his lips could manage that, what a nibble, a lick, a suck could do...?

I swallowed to buy a few seconds time. I did—my body sang with the need for one. But what that looked like? That was where I wasn't quite sure. But wasn't that what a Papa was for? To take care of the pesky thinking for me, to allow me to just be and to feel?

"Maybe?" I went for coy.

"Maybe what?" This time he ended his question with a nip on my earlobe.

"Maybe, Papa?" Damn, that felt right.

His animal growled so loudly inside of him I could hear him.

"My name is Darius, by the way." True mates should know that stuff, right? It was just as important as getting naked, right? And maybe he'd had a hard time hearing the intro, too. Darn us for being in public.

"Nice to meet you, Bunny." He intertwined our fingers together. "Maybe we'd be better off talking not in the middle of a shindig?" I just nodded. "Good. Let's go back to where I am staying."

Not home? I didn't have time to ask, instead allowing him to lead me through the crowd and down a corridor that didn't look like it was there until, suddenly, we were in it. I had a feeling Animals had a lot more secrets than I'd ever be privy to.

Chapter Five

Bruin

I was leading the omega toward my guest suite before I could convince myself it was a bad idea. And making him call me Papa. He didn't object. In fact, I believed he'd done it before I asked. And I'd never played this game before. Sure, I was an alpha and geared to take the lead in romantic situations. But this, taking that alpha one more step into the land of Papa kink, this was different. Darius, in his silly bunny suit, somehow pushed my buttons in a way no omega ever had before and awoke a side of me I hadn't thought to explore.

Mate.

And my pushy bear was right. I never thought to go beyond a little one night of fun because those men, and women on occasion, were nothing more than a good time. I hadn't led them on. Sometimes, people got an itch that needed scratching. Nothing wrong with that.

But since I'd had a taste of Darius' sweet lips and inhaled his intoxicating scent, the thought of anyone else got pushed away. He was mine. And I was his. I must've done something to please the fates to get such a gift.

We reached the doorway leading to the employee and guest rooms, all of which were part of the old shifter cave dwelling. It was magical there, and I wasn't sure if I was allowed to bring someone back without checking first, but decided to beg forgiveness rather than ask permission. If I took long enough to find someone to ask, I'd explode. But I didn't want to fail to ask permission of the most important person in this scenario.

Pausing just outside, where the cool night air whipped around us and the moon shone down, I brought Darius's hand to my lips and kissed it. "Are you sure you want to leave? It's the party of the year..."

He tipped his face up and gave me a small shy smile, the moonlight bouncing off his thick glasses making it impossible to see his eyes, but the words leaving his lips gave ample consent. "Yes, please, Papa. I think I need to go to *bed*." His hand squeezed my ass. I loved how free he was with me while offering his submission. It was a heady mix.

"So you do, do you?" I did, too. There was nothing I wanted more than to sink inside his body and give him my knot and my mark, but I also wanted the evening to last. "I think you're a little *dirty* to be getting into bed so soon. Don't you?" I turned his hand over and gave the palm a critical study, hoping the lines would be enough to distract me from picturing him naked. They weren't. "I think this bunny needs a bath first."

He froze then nodded so hard I was afraid he'd injure his neck. "Does the bath fit two?"

I nodded.

"Do you have bubbles?" How he turned a little question into the sexiest thing I'd ever heard was beyond me.

I had some shower gel that foamed pretty well on the sponge. I thought it would do. *Thank you, Karma, for assigning me the suite with the big bathtub!* "Yes, I have bubbles, but they are only for very good bunnies." I playfully slapped his hand down, the one reaching for my cock. If he did, I'd be as good as done—for a while anyways. I had a feeling with Darius I would be insatiable.

His grin broadened. "I want to be a very *good* bunny, Papa." Reaching for his junk, he pulled me away from the club. "I am a dirty, dirty bunny, though." He went to drop to his knees, and I stopped him. I'd look back on this moment and kick past me's ass, but when I came for the first time, I needed it to be inside of my mate, and I had a feeling his lips held far more magic than the entryway had.

"Well, once we get you undressed, I'll have to inspect and see how dirty you are." My cock throbbed. "Do you want to get naked?" I crossed my fingers the direct statement would undo the flicker of hurt I saw when I stopped him from dropping. "Because I can think of nothing I want more than to see your body void of these clothes, as adorable as you look in them. Your slender body, your firm ass, that cock that doesn't want to stay contained in your clothing, I want to see it all—to lick it all—to explore every inch of you."

He groaned, and it was all I could do to contain myself.

He turned to face me again. "I want it so much."

"Let's go, then." I pulled him to my side. "But since you don't know where we're going, maybe let me lead the way."

I could see him flush even in the night. I could also see his penis jutting straight out from his body, tenting the plush rabbit suit. "Yes, Papa. I forgot I didn't know where to go." From the looks of things, there was a strong chance he forgot a whole lot more. I only planned to make that condition worse.

I suppressed a grin. Did other couples hit it off this fast?

Couples? We'd just met, and I was leaving in the morning. We weren't a couple. But with his fingers curled trustfully in mine, it was easy to toss aside those thoughts. To pretend the man my bear growled was our mate would be with us forever. I wasn't a rolling stone crossing the globe for work, with so little time at home, I was considering selling my townhouse and giving up on pretending I had a base. We'd wake up together tomorrow and the next day and the next.

Or maybe I'd been going about this the wrong way. Instead of running myself ragged and turning down half the jobs available to me because I couldn't fit them in, I should be thinking less like my employee and more like an employer.

"Here we are." We traversed one stone walled corridor then another, taking a left branch then a right. These dwellings went well into the core of the mountain, original caves expanded as the ancient shifters needed more room for their offspring and their offspring's offspring. From what I understood, there were sections the new owners hadn't been in yet, having to concentrate on getting the club going before they had the time to do so. They also took their time, not wanting to damage such precious space. I opened the door to my suite and waved Darius inside.

"It wasn't locked?" he asked, looking nonplussed. "Aren't you afraid someone will break in?"

I guided him inside and closed the door behind me. "How could they break in if there is no lock?"

"I mean...well, come in then, and steal your stuff."

I shook my head. "No, nobody can do that." I led him toward the door opposite and inside the bathroom. "The owners have wards in place that sort out intent. If someone plans to do wrong, they'd never make it into the tunnels."

"Oh." Darius gave a little shudder. "I think I felt something as we came inside. A tingle kind of?"

"Maybe. I've heard some have that reaction as they pass the barrier." I pushed him to sit on the little bench along the stone walled bathroom then turned on the water to fill the deep tub. As the clear liquid splashed into it, the surface revealed gemstones inset, some ancestor's treasure trove cast in smooth concrete or whatever version of it they'd had. Maybe a dragon horde? I thought most of the shifters here in the past were bears, but stranger things had happened.

I planned to use my gel, but then I noticed a jar

marked *Lavender Sandalwood Bubble Bath* sitting on the rim of the tub. Had that been there all along? I had only taken one bath since my arrival, after a day of crawling around on the roof of the club, but I hadn't seen the jar. Perhaps it was a timely offering. "Do you like lavender and sandalwood bubbles, Bunny?"

"No bubble gum scented?" he asked, and I must have gaped because he laughed. "Kidding. I think it would make me gag. What you have there sounds nice, Papa."

I poured a long stream of the silky bubble bath into the tub, and immediately, foam formed. As the level rose in the tub and the aroma filled the air, I turned my attention to preparing the bunny for his wash.

"Stand up, mate." I offered a hand to assist him, and he took it. "Ready to be naked in the bubbles?"

"Yes." He turned around and reached over his shoulder to point to the zipper down his back. "Here's how you open it."

"First, why don't we take off these ears." I lifted them from his head. "No point in getting them wet." I ruffled his hair with my fingertips. "So silky, but we'll need to shampoo it." I grasped the zipper and pulled it down, revealing skin every bit as silky as that hair, and, as I passed the top of his buttocks, I saw no sign of anything under the fuzzy pink suit. “Tsk. You are a naughty . No underpants?” No wonder his cock was so obvious before. “I think it might be a good reason for Papa to give you a little spanking.”

“No, please, Papa. I don’t want a spanking.” Although his tone and the excited quiver in his voice told me the exact opposite.

“How many times did you go out of the house like this?” And please let him continue to do so.

“Uhhh...” He hesitated a moment. “Five times?”

I eased the fabric off his shoulders and down his arms. “Try again.”

“Ten?”

Stroking his bare chest, I took the outfit down to hang around his waist. “Last try. And be honest.”

He began to count on his fingers. I might not know him well but could see it as the theatrics it was. “One thousand, three hundred fourteen.” He was getting into the game. I swallowed a chuckle. “Plus three, Papa.”

“Plus three.” Resting my palms on his hips, I took a seat on the bench and brought him between my legs. “Clever. But I think for a bunny who has been told so many times, and still has a bare bottom”—I pushed the suit over his hips and down his legs to puddle at his ankles—"a reminder is in order—a spanking."

"A spanking?" Darn, he sounded hopeful.

"Lie across my lap here, and we'll get the punishment taken care of before your bath and naptime." I was into this, too.

"Yes, Papa." Darius shifted and bent forward to place himself over my thighs. His bottom stood up high and round, begging for my attention. "Is it going to hurt?"

"What do you think, mate?"

"I think it might. Or it might feel good. Or a combination of both. The books were unclear." So, my sexy omega had researched spankings. I was so going to make it good for him.

I pressed his head down and looked at him lying there, the fuzzy suit tangled around his ankles, his back smooth and straight, skin pale and unmarked. The first spank marred it, leaving a clear print of my hand. He jerked.

"What's wrong?" I rubbed where I'd spanked, ready to continue but wanting to make sure he was still all-in. "Do you want me to stop?"

"Yes...no." He tilted his face to look up at me. "I was naughty."

"And how naughty were you? How many spanks?" I was enjoying this way too much.

"Well, Papa, you told me one thousand, three hundred fourteen and three times."

I bit my lip hard to hold back the laughter. "Too many swats for forgetting to wear your underwear. If I spank you ten more times, will you try to remember next time?"

"Yes, Papa." He faced the floor again, and his cock digging into the side of my leg told me he was as into this as I was.

"Okay, count them out loud."

"I can count to more," he assured me.

"Right, but you only have to count to ten today." I lifted my hand and gave a swift smack across both buns.

"One."

The second was on the opposite side from the first.

"Two."

By the time we reached ten, and his bottom was almost all pink, a trickle down my leg could only be his pre-cum. The little devil. But when I lifted him onto my lap and cuddled him close, a real tear dripped down his cheek. My heart squeezed. "Okay, then, what are we going to remember?"

He dashed away the tear and inhaled deeply before answering, "My underwear."

"Very good."

"Except I don't have any underwear here."

"Hmm. Good point. We'll figure something out. Now, stand up and let's get you in the tub before it overflows and I get in trouble with our hosts."

"Yes, Papa.

Given his reaction, I expected to find all of his underwear suddenly missing.

Chapter Six

Darius

I'd had so many expectations for the night. I was going to dance, to mingle, to live on the edge, and do something I'd never been able to manage before. In my dreams for the evening, I even had my first proper kiss. The reality of tonight outdid my expectations by a million.

First, I scented him. If I'd died right there on the spot, I'd have died a happy man. Then he kissed me. Not a little peck either. We had a full-on, take-your-breath-away, only-seen-in-the-movies kind of a kiss.

And now, I was standing in his place, buck-ass naked, my ass deliciously sore, waiting to take a bath with him. When he thwarted my spontaneous attempt at tasting him, for a nanosecond, I feared he was rejecting me. I still wasn't sure what caused him to decline my unspoken offer, but I wasn't going to complain. Not after he made my wet dreams come true. There was just something about spanking that always did it for me when I watched porn or read a book. Reality surpassed it exponentially.

The scent of the bath mingling with his enveloped me like a hug. A naked hug. A naked hug with a man—no, not a man, my mate. I went from zero kissing to getting ready to being naked in the span of an hour. I needed research or at least a quick search on Google to make sure I didn't get any of this wrong.

"You look nervous." He sidled up to me and cupped my cheek. "If you want me to let you soak alone or if you want us to bid our goodbyes, any of it works for me. Fate sent you my way—no need to rush things."

"You would be okay?" I wasn't sure I was, but to hear him say it was everything.

"Papa bears want what's best for their mates—even if their mates are bunnies."

I was never going to live my bunny costume down. I wasn't sure why I picked it. At the time, it just felt right. And if I was the tiniest of bits honest with myself, I'd have admitted I loved the nickname *Bunny*. As mundane a word as it was, coming from his lips it felt so special, intimate. As intimate as being naked in front of the dressed man.

"Do Papa Bears get in the tubs with their bunnies?" Because bunnies sure wanted them there. Even if said bunny was a bear.

"They do." Nothing more or less.

"Do you get...naked first?" Real smooth.

"Darius, you need to relax. Let me help you in." He held out his hand for me, and I took it. Within a few steps, I was sinking chest deep into the warm aromatic water. The tub at our apartment was a glorified shower. This...this was a tub.

Apartment—Basil. I was the worst friend ever.

"I need to go." I started to get up as my mate was pulling his shirt over his head. "I am the worst friend and roommate ever. Basil is out there all alone, and he didn't want to come. Can I see you again?" Because if I wasn't the picture-perfect example of a cock tease, I didn't know what was. Not that I agreed with that being a thing, but still.

"Whoa, you're going to slip. Sit." He wasn't asking, and, while it was an order, it felt like more. I wasn't going to try and unpack it—not when I was sitting in the tub—because I listened, of course I did, and not while I was naked, hard, and wet. That came out wrong, even in my own mind.

"What are you doing?"

He stood there topless, the button on his jeans popped open, the bulge in the front of them beckoning me to reach out and explore it. He removed his hand from his pocket, his phone coming out as well. "I'm calling the one person I think might have answers for you."

Answers? I didn't have a question. I had a ditched friend, one who I had dragged to the party in the first place. The only questions I might have would pertain to if he would ever forgive me.

"Oh, okay. Thanks." He hung up.

"That was Karma. She said Basil is having a blast and you are to not worry about him." He hadn't asked her anything or greeted her. Had I not sensed his honesty, I'd have called bullshit. "Now where were we?"

"You were getting in the tub with me?" It came out like a question, a question ending with a squeak. "I mean, join me?"

"You are a delight." He unzipped his pants and let them drop to the floor.

"And you are not wearing underwear," I pointed out, trying to contain my giggle at the irony of it. "You just wanted a reason to spank me."

"And you just wanted to be spanked." He wasn't wrong. He climbed into the tub and sat across from me. "It was new, though, wasn't it?" He grabbed a loofa out of a small basket of them on the ledge.

“All of this is.” He was my mate. There was nothing to hide. My face didn’t get the message as my cheeks burned from the embarrassment of it all.

“The tub, too?” He put some soap on the sponge and lathered it up. “Although I can’t imagine most people have an Olympic-sized tub in their bathroom.” He indicated with his finger for me to turn around, and I did, surprised but not upset when he guided me back until I was nestled between his legs. “But that isn’t what you meant, is it, Bunny?”

“Nope. I meant all the things.”

“Are you saying this is your first time with an alpha?” There was no judgement in his words. It was freeing to feel firsthand my answer didn’t matter other than knowing the information. He wouldn’t bolt if I told him I’d been with a bunch of alphas, and he wasn’t going to run when I told him I’d never been with any. Or so my theory went. It was time to omega-up and just say it.

“My first time being with an alpha…in any way.”

“Are you saying you’re untouched?” Was that excitement tinging his voice?

“Today…on the dance floor—” I steeled my spine to say it. “That was my first kiss.”

“A heck of a first kiss.” His breath tickled my ear,

and I felt the loofah on my back for the first time. He wasn't freaking out, which I knew he wouldn't, except self-doubt is a bitch and she was running me hard throughout my confession. "Know this, little Bunny—we are mates. We have our entire lives to get to know each other on all levels. Just because we are shifters doesn't mean we need to move faster than you want."

It sounded so logical to the human side of me. My bear was pushing me to mark our mate already.

"I want a bath, and I want more...but maybe we don't mark each other tonight

"You are such a brave Bunny, telling Papa Bear what you want." He kissed the top of my head. "I have a feeling you are always going to keep me on my toes."

Chapter Seven

Bruin

Darius, or Bunny as he'd become to me, was a revelation. I'd entered the party tonight planning to have a few drinks, visit a while with some of the people I'd gotten to know during my time here, and maybe have a quickie because I was single. And why not? I'd be leaving the next day and was not looking for ties that bind or even a second date.

The realization I was no longer single crashed over me like a tidal wave.

I was mated. My mate had the choice to accept or not, and we were not going to do the actual claiming tonight, but there would never be another for me. In theory, it would be the case for both of us, but theories were just that. If he woke in the morning and told me thanks for the nice evening, have a good life, I would have to accept his decision.

A frisson of anxiety churned in my gut at the thought he might reject me, but as I finished running the loofa over his skin, learning the planes and valleys of his lean form, and splashed handfuls of water to rinse his shoulders and neck, I pushed any nerves and negative thoughts aside. I could not guess what the future held or how I would manage it if he did accept me because it would not change my traveling career. Now would have to be enough for us both. Tonight.

Halloween, when the veils were thinnest and the ancestors who lived within these walls were closest, watching over us. I muttered a quick plea for their assistance if not intercession moving forward.

I rubbed shampoo through his hair and rinsed it with fresh water from the hose attached to the tap before dropping a kiss on his neck. "All right, then. If you will just scoot over to the other side, I'll give myself a quick scrub and we can get out."

"I've never been so clean." Darius moved away from me but not far. Our legs were still touching. "Squeaky clean."

"Then I've done my job as a Papa Bear." Or at least part of it. Anxious to get closer to him again, I completed my own ablutions and rose then stepped out of the tub. With a towel tucked around my waist, and my cock tenting that as it probably would forever, I laid another towel over my arm and reached out a hand. "Get out carefully. All that bubble bath can make things slippery."

Darius laid his hand in mine, and I held tight while he climbed out. "Do you mind my staying over even if we don't...uhhh. You know."

"Shh. It's not all about you know, you know. If you're not ready to take things further, I understand." My dick didn't, but sometimes it didn't get to be in charge. And my bear was all about claiming, but didn't want to scare him off. "Turn around so I can dry your back."

I was already addicted to his body, and I patted the droplets off, starting at his neck and shoulders and working my way down to his flexing bottom cheeks, legs, ankles, feet, then turned him around and did the same with his front. I did have a bad moment when my face was level with his bobbing cock that also seemed to think now was a great time to go to the next level, but with all my self-control, I continued on up until I'd squeezed the last of the water out of his hair.

The thick walls were great sound barriers, and every breath or footfall within the suite was amplified. I'd taken to sleeping with music on because, otherwise, I could hear my heartbeat like something out of an Edgar Allen Poe tale of murder and retribution. With a more romantic atmosphere in mind, as we moved into the bedroom, I hit the switch and turned on the ambient music, something softly classical I'd programmed early in my stay.

"That's really pretty," Darius said. "Kind of goes with the surroundings."

"I thought so, too." I steered him toward the bed and pulled back the covers. "Do you want something to sleep in? I have sweats..." *Please say no.*

"No, I'm...I'd like to sleep, umm...is it okay if I sleep naked?"

Okay? It's amazing. "Sure. I guess I will, too." Like I didn't every night. However, every other night didn't present the challenges of being naked with my mate and not buried inside my mate would. Had he been sent here to teach me patience?

Darius reached for the towel I'd wrapped around his waist and untucked the end, while I watched breathless. I'd have tried not to stare, but such heroics were beyond my abilities. Not fucking him until he was ready was enough of an alpha feat. This omega had not even kissed anyone until tonight, and I had a decade on him, at least. Patience would pay off in the long run.

Hopefully.

When he was lying down, the cock belying his hesitation sticking straight up, I pulled the covers over him and went around to the other side. My towel joined his on the floor before I slid in beside him and lay on my back, trying to be grateful for meeting my mate and asking the ancestors to help me not screw this up. I reached for the switch to turn off the lights that came on automatically when we entered.

I ran over my schedule in my mind. I could stay another day, maybe two at the most if I wasn't going to be late for my next job. With my type of work, I often had to change flights so I never booked anything but business class, and a level where my adjustments could be accommodated by the airlines.

"Bruin?" His voice was quiet in the darkness and seemed very far away.

"Yes?"

"Do Papa Bears mind just cuddling? Even if we aren't going to...you know?" Every time he called sex "you know" he reminded me of his inexperience, that I needed to go carefully and at his pace.

"Papa bears love cuddling." I opened my arms. "Come over here, you snuggle bunny, and let me wrap you up tight and keep you warm and safe all through the night." It was a promise not to do anything he didn't want to do, whether he understood or not. But when he moved into my embrace, I thought he got it. Of course I was turned on, as he was, but sometimes, it wasn't about where we could stick body parts or even giving physical pleasure. My bear, usually the biggest horn dog around, gave a happy rumble as Darius's head landed on my chest.

I closed my eyes and savored his scent, his touch, his soft skin. Sleep wasn't going to come easily, but maybe that didn't matter either.

I could lie here, listen to the music and his breaths evening out, and fantasize about the possibilities the future held for the two of us.

One way or another, we'd make it work.

Chapter Eight

Darius

I rolled over, morning light hitting me on the face long before I was ready to get out of bed. I wasn't sure I'd ever be ready. Being ensconced in his warmth was everything.

I hadn't noticed the window in one wall the night before, since we had traveled so deep in the cliffs. It must look out onto another face. I'd peek when I stood up, see what vista it beheld.

"Morning, Bunny." Bruin kissed my forehead. It was the only kiss he'd given me since we went to bed, and that had me trusting him so very completely. I'd been nervous the night before. So nervous I was shaking. I didn't want to mess things up between my mate and me due to my lack of experience, and the more I thought about it, the worse it got. I planned to research intimacy between alpha and omega when I finally went home. No, not home, the place with my stuff. Home was where my mate was.

And he'd said he was just a guest here...where did he live?

"Morning." My alarm went off from my phone tucked into the hidden pocket in the bunny suit—which I'd left in the bathroom. Darn thing. "It's Friday," I grumbled, the reality of responsibility setting in.

"I was calling today the first day of our forever, but Friday works, too." He squeezed me a little tighter. I liked this sugary sweet side of him.

"I have a class at eleven." Because I was a dumbass and had agreed to cover for Professor Jaymes who thought he might be too tired after taking his five-year-old twins trick or treating. Pretty sure he could've handled it, but it was another case of me trying to fit in where I only half belonged. Saying yes was my way of playing for the team or whatever.

"I really need to learn all the things there are to know about you." He nipped my neck, which made my already painfully hard cock not any better. "I didn't know you were still in school."

"I sort of am, but I'm subbing today." Which I was still pissed at past me for.

"Look at me with a sexy professor as a mate. You don't look old enough to be a professor. I so misunderstood your age." He didn't sound upset by it, mostly confused, and I probably had told him my age at some point. I'd fallen asleep as we talked about all kinds of things from how we ended up at the party to our favorite books. The last bits of the conversation describing myself as awake would've been an exaggeration.

So then I told him all about how I fled my clan under the guise of education and how I adored my mother more than all the stars in the sky, but that even she couldn't convince me to move back. I told him about how I never fit in—anywhere before we met—and how, all of a sudden, I felt like I was where I had always belonged. And by the time round two of my alarm went off, there was no getting around the fact I was going to be late if I didn't get up and leave right then and there. As it was, I would cut it really close, thanks to the long drive ahead of me.

"I wish you didn't need to leave." He handed me a pair of boxers far too big for me. I guess that was a thing for him.

I smiled to myself.

"I'd drive you," he said, "but I need to wrap up things here and, while following you as you drive back is exactly what my bear is begging me to do, finding a new office facility and place to live feels more pressing."

"You are going to stay here—for me?" It had been implied often over the short time I'd known him, yet hearing it spoken out loud added an element of reality to it all. He chose me. His bear chose me. My putting on the brakes hadn't done anything to deter him. He was mine. My alpha.

"We are one now, Darius." He took the boxers from me and bent down, holding them for me to step into and pulling them up my body, gently and not at all sensually tucking me inside of them. "I hope the sweatpants will fit better." He chuckled as I had to grab the underwear the second he let go. He grabbed a pair of sweats off the bed and helped get them on me. "Glad these have strings."

I glanced in the mirror and broke out in a giggle. I looked like a little kid trying on clown pants. I didn't mind. They scented like him, and if I could get away with wearing them to class, I would. "They should stay up like this," I assured him as he tied the strings. "May I have one of your white shirts instead?" I pointed to his company shirt he had sitting on the bed. He looked up at me quizzically. "Then maybe I could wear it as an undershirt to work?" It would look ridiculous with all that fabric tucked underneath my button shirt, but to have him wrapped around me would be completely worth it.

He must've agreed because he was at his dresser fast, grabbing me one.

I was dressed and walking out to the car in five minutes. Papa Bear, or Bruin, walked me to the car, double checking my seatbelt and giving me very specific instructions just as I was about to leave. I was to stay off my cell phone while driving, let him know when I arrived, and, this was my favorite, try not to forget about him while I was gone. As if that could happen.

My bear was livid as I drove away. He pounded inside me, trying to force me back. Thankfully, he had enough sense not to take my skin while I was driving. He'd have to wait. We both would. I arrived with enough time to get dressed, tell my roommate my amazing news, and run out the door. Basil had doubly good news, and it killed me to have to leave before sharing all things with him and the hunk of a man he brought home. It turned out Animals was where we both needed to be last night. Who knew?

Karma, I'd imagine.

I shot off a quick text to my alpha: *I'm here. Miss you already*. I had since before exiting Animal's driveway, but I left that part off.

Not as much as I miss you, omega mine. See you after work?

I was literally counting down the minutes. Was that normal with fated mates? Would it wane over time? Would mating exacerbate or reduce the feeling? I had no answers but was looking forward to discovering them.

We can grab lunch. I added a chicken leg and pizza emoji to my words.

Oh there's something I'd like to grab all right.

I barked out a chuckle as I reached my car. Maybe I could cancel class. It wasn't like the students wouldn't either be skipping or half hungover. There was a reason no other local schools had Friday classes in the first place. Fridays after a day human students used as an excuse to get inebriated only highlighted said reasoning.

Chapter Nine

Bruin

The morning after Halloween at Animals got a slow start. As I did my final checks on the systems I'd put in place, I passed only a dozen or so people, and most looked pretty worn out. Despite the big party, it was Friday and a big night for the club every week, so the place had to be shipshape by sundown yet again. I spotted Warren disappearing into the office hallway off to the side, but Karma was front and center, supervising the various crews in their tasks. I approached her but waited while she spoke to a woman in an apron who was tapping on a tablet as the boss gave her instructions.

Finally, the employee dashed away and Karma faced me. "Oh, Bruin. I didn't think you'd be up this early."

"My mate had to get back to town to teach a class, so I thought I'd be sure everything here was done."

"I see." She cast a glare at a coyote shifter pushing a broom at the speed of a snail then gave me a smile. "And then? Are you leaving today as planned?"

I rolled my eyes. "You know everything, don't you? You tell me."

"I don't know everything. I just thought you two might hit it off." She had the nerve to try to look shocked at my comment, but the twinkle in her eyes revealed her glee. "And did you...hit it off?"

"I said mate, and you heard me. But you set us up, Karma. You invited him here then walked him into my arms."

She shrugged. "I'm a matchmaker, in love with love. So sue me." A loud clatter came from the direction of the kitchen, and she huffed. "I have to go. You'd think I could sleep in for once, but no. Did you want to ask me something?"

"Yeah. I'll be looking for a local home and offices, but is my suite available until I get things nailed down? I have to go out of town in a couple of days, so I hope to have it done by then."

"Such a shame you have to leave right when you met your omega." She tapped a long red fingernail against her lips. "If you're opening an office, though, why don't you give— Do you have a pen?"

I pulled one out of my pocket along with the little notebook I always had on me while working and handed them to her.

"Okay good." She jotted down some notes and handed it back. "That's the name of a young road runner who I think could be a great office assistant for you, and a coyote who already has eco training. I know you have your own methods, but I'm sure they'd love to work for you. He's doing construction while he waits for the right job in his field—your field. And no cartoon jokes if you hire them both."

I tucked the pen and pad back in my pocket. "Karma, I—"

She held up a palm. "Don't say it. It's not magical. A lot of people come through here, and they like to talk to me."

Her mate came up and tugged her to his side, dropping a peck on her lips. "Don't lie to the man." He looked at me. "My wife, my mate is as magical as anyone I've ever met, but she had me fooled with the 'I'm just a human with no magic' crap, too."

"Oh, Warren!" She smacked his chest, but he didn't seem to notice. "Anyway, Bruin, stay as long as you want, and let us know if we can help with anything."

Warren held out an envelope. "Here's your check for the work, and thank you very much. A no-drama contractor of any kind is hard to come by."

I shook his hand and gave Karma a kiss on the cheek before heading for my car and the ride to town. I had researched some things before showering and coming into the club, so I knew where I wanted to look for a place to live. And an office. Buckeye had some real opportunities, including custom-homes builders who could help me create the place I wanted for me, my mate, and, with the grace of the goddess, our family to come. There was also a mixed-use building for sale, with living quarters above office/warehouse space. It was well within my budget and would be a perfect temporary home for us while ours was being built.

I used the travel time to make some calls from my rental car and set up appointments to see the places I had in mind. Real estate probably should take time and serious consideration, but since I'd gone from rolling stone to gathering moss, I didn't want to take any more time than necessary. As in: while I went on my next trip, I wanted escrow happening. The online pics appeared perfect. I had a building inspection license, so if the building suited, I could spend tomorrow checking for problems...

And if my mate liked all these ideas. He'd seemed pretty on the page when he left, but time apart might have taken the shine off.

I sure hoped not.

GPS guided me to his campus, and the guest parking pass he'd promised was at the guard gate, so when he emerged from his class, I was parked and waiting for him.

His smile at seeing me leaning against the bumper told me all I needed to know. And when he stepped into my open arms, it was like coming home. I kissed him, unable to resist his firm, warm lips, but remembering his position, I also tried to maintain some level of decorum and stopped short of stripping him and taking him right there on the trunk of the car, my teeth buried in his shoulder, claiming him.

Laughter behind him helped, and we jumped apart like guilty teenagers. I cleared my throat and cast a quick glare at the laughers. “Ready for lunch, Bun—Darius?”

“That would be nice. Your car or mine?”

I guided him to the passenger door. “Mine. Do you have other plans for this afternoon?”

He settled in the seat, and I buckled him in. “I did, but I called in a favor and cancelled them.”

“Great, so you're free until Monday?” We could see the properties and do other things...as many other things as he was up for.

“A week from Monday. This is the start of fall break.”

Chapter Ten

Darius

"Spain. You're going to Spain?" Basil asked for the third time in as many minutes. Did he think the answer was going to change?

He was at the apartment, picking up a few things he'd left behind when he moved out to be happily mated. I missed him like crazy, but seeing him glow with happiness made it worth it. Of course, the glow could be his little one growing in his middle. That was a thing...I thought.

"Yes. Spain. The Spain. In Europe. The one you take a plane to get to. Spain." I rolled my eyes as I answered him—again.

"Isn't that a little fast?" He was protective of me. But, in his current situation, he hardly had room to talk.

"Says the omega who has a baby in his belly and now lives with his alpha, an alpha he met about a week ago." I snatched his *I'm not responsible for the things I say before I've had my cocoa* mug from his pile. "I'm the only one who uses this."

“Which was exactly why I left it here.” He looked around the mostly barren place. Bruin and I had already packed up most of my things, sorting and donating as we went.

I’d had an inordinate number of used textbooks I’d kept on principle when they offered me five dollars each at the bookstore at semester’s end and eBay searches told me they weren’t lowballing me. Bruin convinced me I should only keep the ones I planned to ever look at again, and had so many boxes of books gone. He also convinced me to keep a few things from my pack, telling me there would come a time when I might wish I had them. I had a feeling that was from experience. Living out of a suitcase had to have been difficult.

“Fair point.”

“So, Spain, huh?”

I pushed his shoulder playfully. “Yes. Spain. I wanted to go to Japan, but, you know, the meeting is in Spain, so off we go.”

“And he’s okay with you being all slow-poky. I mean, this is an expensive trip.” And suddenly, his worry made sense. I was being a slow poke. True. At least by shifter standards. By human standards, we were both rushing things.

“He’s not like that. He knows I am all-in, just I needed a little time to get comfortable with that part.” It wasn’t that I didn’t want to. I thought about it far too often, but fear of doing things wrong or being bad at it had me telling him upfront it wasn’t the night. And then by the time I wanted it to be the night, he was reassuring me it was fine to wait and to not make decisions like that with his tongue down my throat or lapping at my cock. He had a point. Darn considerate alpha.

“This is going to sound weird, but...why don’t you want to?” He set the box of belongings down and leaned against the counter. We were having this conversation. He wasn’t just making small talk. He was such a good friend, even if I wanted to kick his ass out over talking about this. I should be talking about it with Bruin. Maybe this would make it easier?

“It’s not that. It’s...what if I suck, and he’s disappointed?” If the earth opened up and swallowed me whole, I’d have welcomed it. Thinking things like that was one thing. Saying them aloud quite another.

“I guarantee if you suck him, he will not be disappointed.” He winked.

“He might be. You underestimate my lack of coordination and expertise.” I plopped down on the couch and patted it. This conversation would be easier sitting down—or not happening.

"What about after the first time you two kissed?" He pushed himself away from the wall with his foot and came over to join me.

"We went back to his place." I omitted the part about the spanking. It felt too intimate for even a bestie.

"So you kissed him with no experience whatsoever and he wanted more." It wasn't a question.

"Point made." I leaned back, letting my head fall to the fabric with a thud. "We're true mates, and what if..." What if so many things from being a disappointment to not cool enough to ruining his career all came to mind.

"Didn't you just answer your own question? True Mates. That's all you need to know. Fate doesn't fuck around. Packs will let you down. People will let you down. Heck, work will let you down—daily. But true mates? Doesn't happen there." When did he become so confident? Probably a half a second after he got mated.

"You know what? You're right. I'm going to tell Bruin all of my—"

Knock. Knock.

"May I come in?" It was Bruin—two hours early.

Mate.

Pushy bear.

"I'll be going now." Darius winked at me. "I have a mate to get back to. Thanks for my things." He was up and halfway to the door before I even stood.

"Sure."

He opened the door, bantered with Bruin for half a minute, and made his exit. Subtle he was not. Best friend ever—totally.

Bruin stepped in, closed the door, and opened his arms. I walked straight into them, loving the feeling of them wrapped around me.

"So what did you want to tell me?" Because, of course he heard me.

"I was just having omega talk with Basil is all." Lamest excuse ever.

"You do know that's not a thing, right? If you don't want to tell me, it's fine. But if there is something you do need to tell me, know that I will always give you my ear. You come first, from the second I scented you until I take my dying breath. There is nothing you can't say to me, not even goodbye, although to be honest with you, I'd never recover." He spoke softly in my ear, never letting his embrace loosen, keeping me safe and secure in his arms.

"I'm afraid," I confessed in all but a whisper. "Afraid I won't be enough."

Not a breath had passed before his reply came. "You will always be more than. Always."

And, for the very first time, I believed it.

Chapter Eleven

Bruin

I'd postponed the trip to Spain for another week, although I hated to inconvenience the clients. But when Darius and I looked at the building I'd located, we liked it. I spent the next day doing my building inspector act, checking out the roof and the floors, the foundations, HVAC, and all the other details that make a building sound or not, and then made a cash offer. The past decade of working day and night and never taking the time to spend any of the profits had left a good pile of money in the bank. More than enough. So the night before our trip to Europe, we closed on the property. We as in both of us. My mate protested, but from now on, there was no mine and yours, only ours.

It was all done but the claiming.

"This place is so big it echoes," Darius said, pacing from one end of the open-concept living/dining room in our new living space. "And the kitchen is amazing. Why do we need another house?"

"Because I need to have a work life and a personal life separate, now that I actually have a personal life," I reminded him. "The painters and the floor people will be in while we're gone." Also the bathroom remodelers because I wanted him to have a great bathtub big enough for two, even if it wasn't an ancestral pool. But it was a surprise. "Are you sure it was okay to take two more weeks off after the break?"

Darius shrugged. "Yes and no. I am almost done with my dissertation, and they want me to stay here and teach, publish, generally use my brain to raise money with the alums."

He sounded more confident than I'd ever heard him, and I wasn't sure if it was because we were talking about his purview or if our relationship offered a bolster to it, but it really didn't matter. If he was happy, I was happy.

"And you don't mind the sleeping bags tonight? We can go back to Animals and stay." His furnishings, the few he'd kept, were in storage, and mine would be shipped out from my townhouse, which was already on the market.

"Do you mind?" He sidled up to me with a winsome smile. "Because I'd rather stay at our house, if you're okay with it."

Well, it had been my idea after all. "Yes, I'm happy to camp with you."

He'd been keeping things slow all week, but I hoped he'd be ready to complete our mating when we checked into the fabulous villa I'd arranged for our stay. Let's hope he liked surprises because I suddenly loved setting them up. Must be my romantic alpha mode. He liked being pampered, I'd noticed in our first bath together, and I planned to do as much spoiling as he could take.

When we checked in to our villa tomorrow night, he'd find tapas and fine Spanish wine, and the most romantic room my contact there could find for us. I hoped he'd be pleased. Maybe inspired. But even then, I wouldn't push him.

We had a lifetime together.

And my eager cock would have to wait.

We each took a quick shower and climbed into the zipped together sleeping bags. The front wall of windows cast the light from the quarter moon over us. This mostly industrial street was dark enough at night, I realized, we'd be able to stargaze from our bedroom. We'd been sleeping naked every night, challenging me more and more.

"Papa bear?"

I cocked my head at his words. He'd been calling me Bruin for days, except when he was feeling particularly cuddly. As if to prove me right, he snuggled into my arms.

"Yes, Bunny?" He was excited about the trip, his first overseas. "I'm so glad you had a passport already."

"Me, too. I knew I'd go somewhere someday. I pictured maybe speaking at Oxford or Cambridge once I was a full professor."

I stroked his back. "You'll do that, too. Do you mind it not being your first trip?" A few kisses later, I suggested, "You could stay home and wait for the furniture to come...meet the painters?"

"Would a Papa Bear leave his Bunny at home and travel the world?" His pouting tone made me smile.

"Most Papa Bears don't have bunnies..."

"I wanted to ask you something," he said very softly into my ear. "Would you...I'm ready."

"Here? On the floor?"

"On our first night in our home." Darius' voice was a confident as I'd ever heard. And my master plan flew out the window. The villa, the wine, the tapas, they'd be there when we arrived, and we'd enjoy them, but my sentimental omega had chosen tonight to complete our bond. I thanked the fates who sent him to me and then rolled him on top of me and brought my lips to his with no more walls between us.

"I want you to have the best, my Bunny, are you sure?" After we shared a long kiss, the hardwood floor was digging into my tailbone. When I took him, I wouldn't be gentle, didn't have it in me after the wait...

"You, you are the best. And this is our space, whether we are on the floor or up against the wall." His lips curved up in a grin. "That's a thing, right?"

I peppered his face with kisses, moving down to his collarbone and sucking lightly before answering. "It's a thing, and we'll dent every wall in the place, but not tonight." No, and he wouldn't be under me, no matter how traditional it was for the claiming. The room wasn't cold, so I pushed down the sleeping bag and adjusted him with his legs splayed on either side of mine. "We have to catch our flight very early, so it means I can't take all night as I'd like to."

He flattened his palms on my chest and pushed up to glower at me. Cutest glower ever. "Alpha, I'm starting to think you don't want to do this."

My bear had never been so close to the surface. His roar rumbled the floor under us before my teeth pierced the shoulder of my fated mate, going deeper than I thought they should and marking him to us forever. The taste of his blood was coppery and fragrant in my mouth before I pulled back and lapped at the wound, sealing it and assuring it would never fade. I grasped his hips and lifted him over my rigid cock then lowered him, his slick easing the way into his body. Slowly, an inch at a time, I brought him down until he sat on my groin, shuddering.

"I g-guess you do want to." His voice shook, his eyes wide.

I chuckled, eyes half closed in pleasure but not all the way. The moonlight on his face and body cast him in a magical light, one I was feeding into my memory forever. "Are you okay?" I was larger than average, had known that since skinny dipping with the other cubs just moving into adulthood. "Uncomfortable?"

"Full...so full." He wriggled and grimaced. "But aren't you supposed to move around in there?"

"Yes...in time." If I "moved around in there" right now, it would be over in three strokes. "First, I want to see your fist around your cock. Show me how you like to be jerked off."

To his credit, my omega didn't ask questions or protest. He closed his hand around his jutting cock and rubbed up and down, squeezed, stroked his palm over the head, and smeared the pre-cum all around. This wasn't any better. I'd be coming just watching the intent expression on his face.

Okay, alpha. Show your great self-control.

Chapter Twelve

Darius

All of my nerves slipped completely away the second the coppery scent flooded my senses, and I marked him as mine. When he lowered me onto his cock, the fullness awakened something in me—confidence. I had done that. I'd made him hard and needy. I made him scrunch up his nose slightly as his balls tightened, the way he couldn't help but lick the pre-cum he swiped off my tip with his thumb as if it was a gift from the goddess herself. The way he held my gaze as I began to move, slowly at first and increasing in speed as I got the hang of things.

I'd had to bat away his hand a couple of times as I rode him, my need to come too great and his hand paired with his cock making it impossible not to come without getting rid of one of them, and it wasn't going to be the cock.

"You don't like my hand on you, Bunny?" He grabbed onto my hips, guiding me to slow down.

"In the same way you don't like me riding you like the stud you are." My hand came to my face, my attempt at sexy falling flat or off of a cliff possibly.

"You mean you are afraid to come before it's over, Bunny?" I nodded, my cheeks probably twenty shades of red from my bad joke.

"You said we didn't have time to, you know...go all night." I closed my eyes.

Instead of speaking, his hand wrapped around me, giving me a tug with just the right amount of pressure. "Oh we have all night, omega mine. Planes have just been designated for sleeping." He placed my hand on his chest. "How many times do you think I can knot you before the alarm goes off for us to get up? I'm thinking three. It is an early flight, you know."

I bounced up and down, showing my agreement, and we both let go almost instantly, my cum covering his chest, his filling me as his knot grew.

I'd thought him being inside of me was everything. And then I felt his knot.

I fell on top of him, wet and breathless. "Love you." I kissed where I'd marked him.

"And I love you, Darius." He wrapped his arms around me. "Now, rest up because when my knot releases, oh the plans I have for you."

And his plans, including a spanking after all, a little bit of what I called *instructional bossiness*, for it was sexily bossy, and I learned to let go and just feel, and some good old-fashioned snuggling.

We also learned five was the number. It was a good night.

***

"Wanna find out?" And suddenly, I got my confidence back.

"Spain," I answered the TSA agent at Sky Harbor's international terminal for the third time. Were they not listening?

"And the reason for your visit?"

I hadn't gotten to the X-ray machine for my bag, and they were already giving me garbage. I didn't get it. I had a passport. I had a ticket. I had one small suitcase. What was their problem?

"I am going with my ma—boyfriend on his business trip." Again, information he knew.

"And the name of your hotel?" He tapped his pen against my ticket, the ticket that felt like it was getting farther and farther outside of my reach.

Bruin had already passed through this area and, at their repeated instructions, had "moved along." I had no inkling of doubt he was waiting for me, watching the entire thing. Had it been anything other than security, he'd have probably already intervened by now. It wasn't as if I had done anything wrong.

"I told you that, too. I don't know. My boyfriend said it was a surprise." Calling him boyfriend felt like a lie. He was so much more. But humans, and our agent was human from all I could scent, didn't have an equivalent word. The closest they had was marriage, and that required legal things we just hadn't done. Probably should since we bought a house in a human community.

We. That was still weird, too. I'd contributed a grand total of $1000, and getting him to accept such a small amount had been a challenge. It was money I'd been saving up for a fancy new computer, and he said I shouldn't sacrifice. I pouted and won the battle but had already seen the ads showing up on his phone for computers. He'd been looking, so did I really contribute? Still, he'd insisted it was *we,* and, after our night together, it felt very much *ours*.

"You really should know your plans." He sighed, handing me my ticket, and leaned in slightly. "If your mate weren't pretending not to glare at me as waves of worry pour off him, I'd have thought you were a possible concern." Huh, so not human. Or possibly human in the same way Karma was. So yeah, not human.

"Thanks. He's trying to be romantic." I rolled my eyes, the tension in my shoulders slipping away.

"I'd keep him. Now, move along. The line is growing." He wasn't kidding. Lucky we'd arrived early.

He didn't need to tell me again, I scurried off and, after a quick run through the machine, found myself in my mate's arms.

"What was that about?" He kissed the top of my head. "I was getting worried."

"You and me both. Let me get my shoes on, and I'll tell you all about it." I gathered my things, and we headed towards our gate. We had a couple of hours to kill, but I wanted to know where we were needing to be. It was my first international trip and only my second by airplane, the first being a few years earlier when I went to present a paper to our sister university. This trip was going to be far more fun.

"Hungry?" he asked, tilting his head in the direction of the only restaurant in view of our gate. "It might be nice to grab a table instead of eating on our laps." Papa Bear knew me so well, even if we were still discovering something new about each other constantly and not even necessarily the deep stuff. I'd only learned his favorite color was green a day ago.

"Sure."

We walked hand in hand, our little carry-on bags rolling behind us, to the hostess station, where the man seated us quickly in the back corner. I could still see the gate-ish, but we had some privacy. I loved it.

Bruin sliding into my side of the booth had us getting some side-eye from the hostess, and it gave me a small case of the giggles as she walked away. Stress relief from the security bits, I'd gather.

"So what had you looking so suspicious to the agent?" Bruin's arm wrapped around me, and I leaned into him. "Or was he looking for a sexy omega? Because if so, this one is taken."

His thumb brushed my mating mark, and my mind raced back to our mating, and how sweet, gentle, yet in charge he was. How I didn't have to worry about anything because Papa Bear had it all under control. How I'd never felt more cherished in my life. Probably not the best train of thought given we were in public. At least the table hid my reaction from the world. Not from Bruin, though, and it felt deliciously naughty when his hand slipped over my growing bulge and gave it a knowing pat.

"Hardly. He didn't like that I didn't know anything

about the trip other than Spain." Which was dumb given he saw I was traveling with another. And really, if I were up to no good, wouldn't I have a story made up to fill in the blanks.

"Good to see they take security seriously. Wish it wasn't at the expense of my nerves." He forced a chuckle. "I will tell you next time."

"Or tell me now, in case they ask again in Spain?"

The waitress came with waters, interrupting our conversation long enough to take our order of burgers and fries.

"So, alpha mine, tell me about Spain or at least the hotel—no tell me about Spain."

"It will ruin the surprise. Are you willing to have it be like Christmas morning when you already know your gifts?"

Had I had one of those? "I'll take my chances."

"We are not staying in a hotel room." He removed his arm from around me to retrieve his phone from his pocket. "I rented us a villa."

"Ohhh, you spoil me." And I loved every second of it.

"You have no idea the plans I have, omega mine. You have no idea."

But I was about to find out.

Chapter Thirteen

Bruin

When we were finally settled in our business class seats and on the way to Spain, my omega rested his head on my shoulder and fell asleep. I didn't blame him. We'd probably gotten an hour's rest the night before, despite my intent to do so. And it wasn't the hard floor that kept us awake.

My mind moved back to our first time together. His mating mark glowed in the moonlight as I used my grip on his hips to raise and lower him, my cock deep in his body then out almost all the way, again and again. It hadn't been three strokes, but neither had it been long enough. Luckily, my mate's busy hand rubbed him into spurting his cum all over both of us, a fountain of creamy goodness adding more gleam to his skin under me.

The shreds of my control fell away, my cum flowing into him then my knot swelling to hold it in place. Had we created a cub? I thought it would be nice to have time alone together, but the idea of a young one of our own made my chest swell with pride.

Whenever I closed my eyes, I could see it, my omega rounding with our young.

"Sir?

I blinked, waking from a dream I hadn't realized I'd fallen into. A good one, though. I stretched, only then realizing I was alone. Where was my omega?

"Sir, we'll be serving lunch in a few minutes and I wanted to know if you wanted chicken or beef?" Lunch. I'd slept a long time.

"Beef, I guess." This airlines tended to have dry chicken dishes.

"And do you know what your companion would like?"

"Same." He must be in the bathroom, but when he reappeared and sat down just as the flight attendant was reaching our row with trays, Darius looked way too excited to have just gone to the restroom.

"I ordered you the steak for lunch, hope it's all right."

"Sure." He leaned back to allow the attendant to set my lunch on the tray table then lowered his own. "Looks good."

"We are halfway to Spain."

He probably knew, but I was trying to figure out how to ask what had him so smiley.

"Great. I just ran into a professor from my university who is headed to Madrid to deliver a paper I did research on for him. Isn't that exciting?"

"It is!" I forked up a piece of steak. They still served the good cuts, but they came pre-sliced since knives had become a no-no. "What's the topic?"

He explained all through lunch and dessert—apple crisp with ice cream—but when he finished, I still didn't understand, really. I was a science guy, and my omega liberal arts. "So this document was so obscure nobody had been able to translate the version of Old English before, and Prof is up for three or four awards for his work. For our work..."

"Omega, does it bother you he's getting credit for what you did?"

He bit his lip. "A little, but once I finish my doctorate, I will be doing more things on my own. And my thesis focuses on another recent find I am confident will add to the conversation in a meaningful way."

"Well, good." He would be famous in his own right. I had no doubt. As the trays were cleared away, I spotted a man in his sixties sporting a Hawaiian shirt and khaki shorts, standing behind the flight attendant. "Is this your friend?"

"Professor Dunham." Darius' grin told me he didn't resent the man at all. "I'd like you to meet my mate, Bruin."

The prof held out a hand, and I shook it. "Nice to meet you, Professor. I understand you're involved in some exciting work."

Okay...way to turn on an academic. Not only did he proceed to tell me all about it in detail, plopping down in the currently vacant seat opposite us, but my omega chimed in. An hour or so later, I realized the man who'd been sitting there had never returned. I craned my neck and spotted him several rows up, probably in the professor's spot.

The rest of the trip, I read magazines while Darius and Professor Dunham engaged in a spirited exchange of ideas. While the topic was not one I could follow or really tried to, it was a pleasure to see my omega in his element.

When the seatbelt light came on again and the pilot announced we'd be landing soon, the two sat back and sighed. "Best flight ever, son," the older man, who I'd figured out during their conversation was a feline shifter, said then addressed me. "I should apologize for monopolizing your omega, but he's one of the best and brightest, as you probably already are aware."

"He's special in a lot of ways," I told him.

"I'm glad you recognize that." He hesitated before continuing. "The conference I am attending is very important in our field. Would you have any objection to his joining me for the next couple of days?"

I startled. This alpha wanted to kidnap my omega right after our mating? My bear was not happy.

"I don't know..."

"It's a great opportunity," he went on then winked. "And we would only be away from you during the day. Unless you'd both like to attend the closing banquet."

Suppressing my jealousy, I tried to think like the good kind of alpha, the kind who wanted their omega to succeed and be happy and put their needs first. "Darius, do you want to go?"

He turned shining eyes on me, his whole face alit with happiness. "Do you mind?"

"Not at all," I lied. "I can get started on my project right away, so you would have been bored anyway." And that part was true. "Would you like me to accompany you to the banquet?"

"Yes, I would love it." Despite the professor, he peppered my face with kisses. "You're the best alpha ever."

Dunham chuckled. "My omega comes along when

he can, but his surgery schedule doesn't always allow it. I admire his dedication to his career, but sometimes it annoys my leopard."

I got it. I totally did.

Chapter Fourteen

Darius

"Did you enjoy your vacation, love?" Bruin turned the car into the driveway of our new home. In theory, it now had furniture in it, but I knew from moving the few times I had that furniture did not mean livable, and I was dreading it.

"Words cannot describe how much." Maybe it was because the people in attendance weren't the same people who watched me grow up on campus, but I felt so at ease with my peers—for many of them were and the others at the conference would soon be. I was so professionally refreshed, something I'd needed. "Thank you for letting me do all the boring stuff," I sassed. It wasn't boring, and Bruin had never hinted it might be. Sure, compared to our knottings it was tame, but everything else on the planet would be, too. Sex was that good.

And to think I was so nervous about it. Or maybe the anticipation was what made the first time so amazing. No. That wasn't it. Bruin was what made it so amazing then and every time since. There was nothing comparable to the feeling when the two of us were bonded together by his knot.

"I'm glad. I was afraid it would be a letdown given I had to work."

Not sure how he ever could've thought that. He had planned tours, dinners, art galleries, and the most beautiful place for us to stay. I didn't need any of it to be content, only to be in his arms, but I enjoyed every second of it.

"You could never let me down, Papa." My bear growled in agreement as he put the car in Park.

"Your bear likes me." He turned off the ignition and gave me a kiss on the cheek. "We need to let them out to play."

He wasn't wrong. It had been so long since I'd let mine out between being in the city and feeling like an outcast to bear kind, I kept pushing his desire to roam back. I'd not been fair. Had I a will, I'd have been able to make it happen.

"Agreed. Mine hasn't been out in too long." I sighed as I reached for the door handle. "Do you think it is safe here?" We'd, or I should say Bruin, had picked this place as one for us to consider based on location, but that didn't mean our animals had free rein. We weren't on clan land.

"If we don't wander too terribly far. All of the closest neighbors are shifters."

"Which doesn't mean all of the people here at any given time are—got it." I climbed out of the car, excited to see the place. Furniture, paint, and, in theory, a fancy-schmancy bathroom awaited me. Bruin had let his surprise on that front slip one night. I had a feeling the last part wasn't done. Remodels always took too long. It was a rule or something.

We walked into the unit, and I just stopped, jaw dropped open. The transformation blew my mind. It had been gorgeous when I first saw it, but now? Now, it looked like something out of a home magazine. The walls were both painted and stenciled, the floors beautiful hardwood, the furniture both eclectic and inviting. Whomever did the work managed to have my favorite chair in the mix and not looking like the last item needing replacing.

"Wow!"

"That good?" He scooped me up in his arms. "Wait until you see what awaits." He carried me to what I knew to be our bedroom and pushed the door open with his foot. It was like a luxury hotel, only homey. From the four poster bed to the granny quilt to the matching nightstands—it was more than I could've dreamed of.

"I love it. How? When?"

"I made phone calls when you were being all impressive and smart." He kept walking in the direction of the bathroom. "They didn't love the weird time zone difficulties. What can you do? Now close your eyes, Bunny."

I squeezed them shut as he held me closer, maneuvering us into the bathroom, which still smelled of paint and caulk. "May I look now?"

"May I look now what?" His voice deepened and his scent intensified.

"May I look now, Papa Bear?"

He set me down. "You may."

I cracked open my eyes, and, while the bathroom had been completely redone, my eyes were glued to one thing—the tub. It was exactly like the tub at Animals. Exactly.

"How?"

"I have my ways." He pointed to a hook beside the tub. It held a pink bathrobe and below it a pair of bunny slippers. I couldn't help the giggle escaping me.

"Want to try it out?"

"More than anything, but unfortunately, they just finished today and they want it to sit for another twenty-four-ish hours. I have something else we can do in here, equally intimate." He nibbled on my ear and walked around me to the sink, which had a lunch-sized paper bag sitting on it. He snatched it up and handed it to me. "Amuse me."

I took the bag and opened it up, expecting something for sexy times and instead finding not one, but four pregnancy tests, all different brands.

"You think I'm pregnant?" The thought had crossed my mind a few times, sure. I had yet to feel any symptoms, though, so I figured it was just daydreaming.

"My bear does."

That caught me off guard. I knew bears sensed these things first, I'd just always assumed it was the bear of the prego guy. And maybe that was my "daydreaming," my bear trying to tell me. The darn thing had words. He needed to use them. I was not good at subtlety.

"Since when?" And why wasn't mine doing more than hinting? I was actively trying not to get my hopes up. But a baby. A sweet little mini-me of Bruin. Nothing in this world could make me happier.

"Since the flight to Spain." I gave him the *you better keep talking* finger swirl. "When security got weird, he was clawing at me to save our babe. I thought he meant you, but he keeps saying the word—babe."

I was pregnant. My bear's mate would know, and if he was that adamant, there had to be a reason. Right? And then there were my random thoughts of being pregnant. I was having a baby. Bruin's baby. Probably. Those tests called to me.

"Will you be all right if you are? I mean, your career and all." Oh, how he misinterpreted the expressions that must've accompanied my inner monologue.

"I would be more than all right." I threw my arms around him, peppering his face with kisses. "All I've ever wanted is a family who accepts me, and here you are making that possible."

His hands on my shoulders stopped my bouncing, and he waited until I met his eyes to begin speaking.

"I don't just accept you, Bunny. I love you with my whole heart. I am honored to know you, more to be a part of your life. I am proud of you—so very proud. And not gonna lie. Knotting you doesn't suck either."

"Doesn't suck, huh?" I pushed him playfully as I tried in vain to blink past my tears of joy.

"Nope." He accentuated the P with a pop.

"Let's do this thing." I grabbed the bag and opened the boxes one by one. Within five minutes I had four positive pregnancy tests laid out on the counter.

"We're having a baby." This time it was Bruin with the unshed tears. "A baby."

"I'm going to be a dad." I placed hands on my belly.

Run.

"And my bear is being an ass. He wants out with his mate to celebrate."

"Then fur it is." He took me by the hand and led me to the back door where we barely got our clothing off before our bears took over, enjoying their first run together and the excitement of our growing family.

So much better than a bath.

Chapter Fifteen

Bruin

How quickly things moved from Halloween night when I met my omega. I'd been bopping along, being single, working too hard, and focused on nothing else except occasional regrets about leaving my clan behind. Perhaps that contributed to the workaholic thing. And I'd worried about Bunny thinking it was odd, an alpha making the decision I did, to leave rather than fight. But when I told him, he only said, "I'm so glad you were where you were that night to meet me. It wouldn't have happened if you'd chosen otherwise. Fated mates, Papa Bear. We had to be where we were when we were for everything to come together just as it needed to."

Fated mates. This was exactly what the phrase meant.

Living above my business was great for now. For a mixed-use/mostly industrial neighborhood, it had a large shifter population, and when all the businesses closed, the people who actually inhabited the apartments and lofts came out and mingled. Lots of pot lucks and barbecues on Sundays right in the middle of the street waiting to be clogged with delivery trucks on Monday. Our home was being built outside of town, but it wouldn't be ready until after the baby came, so we'd added a nursery nook to our bedroom.

Hiring both the people Karma recommended and a few others as well had made it possible for me to travel only for a few days here and there to get jobs set up or help with difficult projects, and as my omega swelled with our child, I tried to make those trips few and far between.

Our doctor and midhusband shared a practice and were the nicest, most caring people I'd ever had the pleasure to encounter in the medical field. They were also mated, and their toddler and his manny were often there when we visited.

"Ready to go, Bunny?" I wanted to get to our ultrasound appointment a little early. "We need to hit the road soon."

Darius groaned from the bedroom. "I...can't...button these jeans. Go without me."

I could feel my eyes roll. "Wear the daddy jeans we bought. They should fit fine."

"Not yet," he wailed. "I don't want to be so fat yet."

"Omega." I waited a moment, but he didn't

respond. "Omega, if we're late, they won't be able to fit us in. You know how popular your doctor is. Put on the pregnancy pants. What are you saving them for?"

He emerged a moment later, wearing the new pants. "You should have to get fat, too."

And he sailed past me to the stairs and descended out of sight. Omega bears almost always thickened when they were pregnant, not just in the belly but all over, and my mate was no different. But sometimes it bothered him, probably because he was unusually lean for our type and even his sleeves were tight. It was a transformation he might not have been ready for, and I made a mental note to get the older bear omega who came to all the BBQs and was steeped in wisdom to talk to him later.

I grabbed a couple of water bottles and followed him down and out to the van. Darius was almost always easygoing, but pregnancy hormones had brought out a pensive, occasionally snappy side to him. Though I'd grown up around pregnant bears, I'd left the clan young enough I wasn't really interacting with them, so this was on-the-job alpha training in the care and feeding of my mate.

We arrived in plenty of time after a silent ride, and I went around and opened Darius's door, closing it after he climbed down, ignoring my extended hand. I got it—he was "fat" because of me, and my reassurances I found him sexier than ever only seemed to upset him. When the office door was locked, the *out to lunch, back soon* sign still in place, he turned on me with an expression capable of melting my face off.

I almost took a step back, but then my bear rumbled and reminded me of something important. As the alpha, it was my job to step in and take charge when my omega was emotionally on the rails. Bring things back on an even keel. Meet my omega's needs whatever they were. And in trying not to set him off, I'd been contributing to his running amok. Not good for him. Not good for me. Not good for our cub.

A bench sat under a shade tree a few feet away, and I took Darius by the scruff and guided him there, pushed him gently down to sit.

He glowered at me, but did not stand up again.

Not really progress.

I loomed over him for a moment, prepared to growl and snarl and tell him to get his act together when I saw how wrong that would be. Behind the glare lay a whole other emotion. How would I feel if my body was suddenly changing? If I had not only the changes every pregnant omega went through but those faced only by ursine shifters? He'd lose the baby weight, but not the structural changes. He'd have bigger arms and legs, a thicker waist, and probably would be a little taller.

Sinking to sit beside him, I took his hands in mine. "It sucks, doesn't it?"

He didn't reply, but he did cock a brow, at least responding.

"Everything must feel so out of control. And though we're in this together, I get to parade you around and brag about our wonderful new family on the way, while still wearing the jeans I always have and being able to rely on my body to behave as it always has. I can't imagine what it must feel like to change so dramatically, but I want to try."

He gave a slight nod. "I-I'm scared, Papa Bear."

My heart broke for him, but I couldn't join him in the emotional depths. I had to bring him out of them by staying there. "What scares you the most, Bunny? Tell me so I can help."

"How can anyone help?" A tear trickled down his cheek. "What if something is going wrong? I feel like I can't count on my body anymore. It's all stretched out and swollen and nothing fits. Not even my shoes." I followed his gaze down to see he was wearing slippers.

How had I not noticed? "I'm not throwing up anymore, but I still feel nauseous about half the time, pee a thousand times a day..." Once the dam broke, there was no stopping it. Or the tears accompanying it. I wanted to hug him to me and pat his back, soothe him, but I didn't. He needed to get it out.

And thinking back, I had to take some blame for the bottled-up emotions spilling over. Every time he got upset, I cuddled him and told him to shush, it would all be fine soon. I hated him being anything but happy, so when he seemed down, I swooped in and petted him until he smiled. Then, when that stopped working, I backed off and tried not to do anything to make him more upset.

I didn't "alpha."

So this time, I listened. And didn't try to stop his tears, just held his hands while he let it all out. And when he finally stopped, and took a deep breath, I said, "Okay, I hear you. Let me see if I understand your biggest concerns, all right."

"Okay." But he looked doubtful.

"You are worried about the changes you're going through, whether they are normal for a pregnancy, and you feel unwell a lot of the time?"

"Yes."

"But knowing you, and knowing how caring you are and loving, I think the thing you mentioned the least is the one occupying your mind most often. You want to be sure everything with the baby is going okay, that none of these symptoms you're experiencing mean the cub is in any trouble."

He blinked, licked his lips. "Do you think something is wrong? What if I'm eating too much and it's causing the baby to be sick? Or not develop right? What if I'm already a bad father?"

"Oh, Bunny. You're the best father. No baby could be more loved."

And now I cuddled him close, rubbed his back and spoke low in his ear a whole different variety of love words than ever before, but more meaningful. "Darius, you already eat healthy, and if you have the occasional treat, it's fine. When we go in to see the doc, we're going to ask a lot of questions to make sure we are *both* on track, and your body is, as I already believe, doing just what it should. I promise to be there for you whenever you need me, but to do that, I need a promise from you."

He sniffled against my shirt. "O-okay. What do you want me to promise?"

"That you hold me to mine. If you ever feel like

I'm not listening, not meeting your needs, you'll call me on it. Though the physical changes are all on you, the rest needn't be."

He leaned back, his face still woeful, but no longer resentful. "So you aren't mad because I've been so grouchy?"

"Mad?" I grabbed him again and gave him a big squeeze. "Not in a million years. And you aren't mad because I've been missing all the cues I should have been catching?"

"Yes."

I gaped.

"Kidding. But if you feel guilty, you can buy me a sundae on the way home."

My grin stretched my cheeks, and weeks of tension left my shoulders. "What about eating healthy?"

"I'll get a banana split. Fruit."

Just then, a sedan pulled up, and the doctor and midhusband emerged.

"Looks like time for our appointment." Darius stood and bent to drop a kiss on my cheek. "Lucky we got here early, huh?"

I rose and took his hand. "Yep. Let's go get a look at our baby. Do you want to know the sex?" We'd gone back and forth on the topic, never reaching a conclusion.

"No. Let's make it a surprise."

I started toward the door held open by our midhusband, Andy. "Whatever works for you, Bunny. But I am curious."

"Hello, you two," chirped Andy. "Sorry we're late. I hope you weren't waiting too long."

We smiled at each other then at him. "Just long enough," Darius said. "So, how does this work?"

Ten minutes later, my Bunny lay on the table, his shirt pulled up and his belly gleaming with the gel that would allow the device Andy called a "transducer" to move over his skin and capture the images soon to appear on the screen. I held my omega's hand as Andy asked, "Are we going to find out the sex?"

I parted my lips to say no, but Darius beat me to the reply. "Absolutely."

"All right, then."

I looked from the moving device to the screen and back again. Then, it stopped. "There he is."

If kissing an omega on the exam table was a problem, neither Andy nor his alpha doctor mate who came in just then commented. In fact, they kissed, too.

Papa Bear for Darius

We were having a son. Now we had to think of names...

Chapter Sixteen

Darius

"He should've had his shower two months ago like a normal person. Who has a shower on their freaking due date?" I huffed as I tried once again to get my socks on before Basil's shower was over. I was on attempt four. I wasn't growing a baby, I was growing a teenager—I swore it. "Are you going to help or what?" I gave up, throwing my sock at my alpha like an impudent child and instantly regretting it. "I suck. Can I have it back? I can do this." I conceded.

"Absolutely not, Bunny." He knelt in front of me, or at least I assumed he did. I couldn't see him over my huge belly, and I still had over a month to go. "This is my job. You grow the cub, and I do all the rest."

"Doesn't sound fair to me."

He gave my foot a rub then slid on the sock. It felt amazing.

"It isn't fair, omega mine. But it's the least I can do,"

"That's not— Never mind." No sense going around the conversation again. He'd win. He always did. It was par for the course with the irrationality that set in during my pregnancy. At least I *mostly* saw it for what it was after it spouted from my mouth. I still hadn't figured out how Bruin put up with it all.

"Let's get your shoes on and head to the shower." He helped me up from. the bed, and we headed to the door where my slides lived. Shoes were a big no with my feet the size of the shoe boxes.

"I hope they like the baby carrier." The salesman said he could exchange it for another if it wasn't comfortable, but I still wanted Basil to love it. It was adorned with octopuses, his favorite.

"He is going to like whatever you got him because you got it with love." My mate, a cheesy greeting card on legs. Goddess I was a lucky omega.

We drove to Animals, and of course, I had to pee five minutes out. By the time he pulled up to the entrance, I was ready to jump out of the moving car to get to a bathroom.

"Let me out here," I pleaded.

"Meet me in the coatroom, okay?"

I popped out of the door as fast as my whale of a self could. "Sure."

Had I known his reason, I'd have given him a what for—or seven.

By the time I made it out and to the coatroom, I could feel something was up. I could scent Basil and a bunch of others were there, yet the place was suspiciously silent.

"What is going on?"

"You said no shower. Basil said fuck that. Here we are."

My jaw dropped as the pieces fell into place. I had said no shower a bazillion times. We had all we needed, and the further along in my pregnancy I got, the less I enjoyed peopling in groups.

"Now, slap on your best surprised face." It was an order, and my bear submitted, making the entire walking in so much easier. Bruin knew what I needed—once again.

"Yes, Papa." I took his hand. "Tonight, maybe we can just be slugs?"

"Tonight, we will just be slugs."

He led me around the corner and into the VIP room where everyone and their brother shouted out, "Surprise!" Only when it came time for me to act surprised, it was no act. Instead, I bent over in pain, my legs suddenly drenched. This wasn't supposed to happen. I'd read all the books—all of them. This was not how it was done. It wasn't.

Except it was.

"Something's wrong." So very wrong.

"I've got you, Bunny. I've got you." The rest of the room faded away as he gathered me up.

People were talking in the *whamp whamp whamp* of cartoon voices as I shut my eyes, willing the pain away, not having the ability to ask a question or even cry out. It was too much.

The next thing I knew, I was being place on something soft—a bed—yes, a bed, and I felt a prick in my arms seconds ahead of things growing more clear. As I opened my eyes, I saw both my lifelines—Bruin and my doctor. What the...?

"I don't remember being in the car." My words were barely audible.

"Karma invited him, and for some *strange* reason, he agreed."

Yeah strange reason all right.

"Am I...? Is the baby...?" I couldn't even say the words. The pain was gone, but that didn't mean anything other than I could focus enough to ask the questions.

"Everything will be fine. Your little guy decided to shift early. An alpha to be sure."

Shift. Shit! Babies don't shift, and not in the

womb.

"I can't deliver a bear cub!" I tried to sit up, and Bruin held me firm with the look promising trying it again would result in the same.

"You need to stay still while we work on getting him to shift back," the doctor chided. "And with Andy attending to Basil, I need to not worry about you being pushy on this."

"Basil?"

"He is in labor but didn't want to miss your shower," Karma explained as if that was the normal way to go about life—living your day normally while you tried to push out a babe.

I hadn't scented her entering the room, come to think of it. My ability to scent was worth shit. Brilliant.

"His shower," I corrected. Because I was getting my feisty back.

"The shower." She tsked. "How about that?"

"Fine." And my arm pinched again. This time I saw the culprit, a needle.

"You distracted me on purpose," I accused, and she shrugged, turning on her heel and going who knew where. Heck, I wasn't sure exactly where I was.

"Is the ambulance coming?" Because I needed to get to a hospital or something. I was not having my baby in a bar or club or home or ugh. Animals was everything. I still wasn't going to have my baby here.

"For you to give birth to a bear? Yeah, that would go over well," Karma called from farther away. Hadn't she left yet?

"We have everything we need here. I just needed to chill your cub out a bit, so your mate can force his change." He spoke so calmly and so undoctorly. He hadn't been like this at our appointments. Of course, those had been in facilities with humans, so maybe this was the difference?

"You say it likes it's no big deal." I bent my knees and used my feet to skootch myself up, hoping to get a better view of my surroundings. "I have a cub with claws inside of me." And all of the things I read about ruptured uteruses started to replay in my head—the last thing I needed, especially in a strange bedroom and not a hospital.

"Not for long." His palm came down on me gently, settling on my hand. "He's sleeping now." That calmed me. Slightly. But then he had to go and ruin it by turning to my mate and saying, "Wanna do your thing, Papa Bear?"

Cause heck to the no.

I growled.

No. My bear growled.

Loudly.

"Don't. Call. Him. That!" I sat up. Nobody would've been able to stop me. The only thing keeping my bear from ripping through me was my baby. It was fair to say my irrationality had amplified. It was only a phrase. Sure, I used it to be more, but still. That didn't stop me from seething as I barked, "He's *my* Papa Bear."

I swore the man had the patience of a saint because, instead of letting his animal come to the forefront at my not-so-subtle challenge, he shrugged, bared his neck, turned to my mate, and said in the calmest voice I'd ever heard, "Wanna do your thing, Bruin?"

I didn't know if it was his calmness, the medicine he'd injected me with, or magic, but something sated my beast, and I lay back down. My cub needed this. I needed this. Losing my shit for no reason wasn't helping anyone.

"Close your eyes, mate." He placed his hand on my belly and closed his own because, yeah, I peeked. It wasn't instantaneous, but, after four deep breaths, things changed. It was a cross between when my cub did karate in my middle and when he dropped, but all in one swoop. He was a babe again. I could feel the difference.

"I felt that." I placed my hands on my mate's.

"Good. It means it worked." He leaned down and spoke to our son. "You stay just like that, okay, son? We need you to come out so you can take your fur again."

The doctor cleared his throat. "So how about we get this baby out of you before he decides to take his fur again?"

If only it were so simple. My concerns over it being too soon were easily countered with *if he can shift, he is ready*, and once I let it sink in, I did my best to help my little guy come into this world—including helping my mate take a bath, pacing around the room with him, and begging him, although more out of desperation than anything else.

Three hours later, after forty-five minutes that felt like a decade of pushing, our sweet baby boy was born at, as I later learned, the same exact minute as Basil's, according to the midhusband's report. We later teased that they were *the twins*.

"You did so good, Bunny." Bruin settled in beside me, our babe on my chest, eating for the first time. "He's perfect."

"He needs a name." We'd talked about so many over the months, but none of them felt right.

"Coello." And there was Karma again, this time with her mate who never seemed far from her. They pretty much orbited each other.

"Co what?" Bruin asked, his eyes never leaving our son.

"Coello. It's Galatian. Means Rabbit. You're Welcome." And she was off.

"Coello?" I asked, and our babe stopped nursing to look in the direction of my voice. "Coello."

"Coello," Darius agreed. Our little rabbit.

Epilogue

Bruin

We spent the first week of Coello's life at Animals. Back in the guest suite where we'd first slept together, but this time, we were a trio. All the baby shower gifts made us lack for nothing, but we mostly stayed because Karma, our matchmaker, insisted. She pointed out her staff would wait on us hand and foot, as well as Basil and his mate, Chris, in the suite next door. The hallway was packed with people carrying trays, bringing more gifts, and just popping in to get a peek at the babies.

Turned out, while the omegas were laboring, those who'd attended their shower were dancing, drinking, and generally carousing in a new ritual they declared necessary for good luck for the new parents. But if you're going to give birth on the grounds of a night club, you could probably expect a party. And in a way, it was sweet. Unable to resist, I'd taken the new baby just inside the door of the club and held him up, announcing the birth of the new bear prince. Technically, only the prince of our home, but you'd never have known it from the cheers. It was a day I'd never forget.

But at the end of the week, it was time to go home. Not that the gang at Animals didn't try to keep us, but we needed our space, our privacy, and peace and quiet. Plus, as Darius pointed out, we had an amazing nursery alcove just waiting for the baby.

I carried them both over the threshold, up the stairs, and to the bedroom where I set my omega and the baby in his arms on our bed.

He looked around, a happy smile tipping up the corners of his mouth. "I don't know why we need the house we're building. I love it here."

"You say that now," I replied, sitting next to him and stroking Coello's soft cheek. "But in a couple of years we're going to be very happy to have a big yard. Our guy wants a swing set."

"And a puppy." Darius bent close to the baby and cooed. "You want a puppy, don't you, little guy?"

A puppy. "Maybe we should wait on the puppy, until he's old enough to take care of it."

"And a kitten because the puppy needs a friend." Darius was completely lost in his chat with our son, now, telling him about all the pets we'd have, and the biggest swing set on the block. How we'd travel with

Daddy when he went on trips sometimes and see the world.

I wanted them to see the world. Wanted the whole world to see them. The most amazing omega and beautiful baby ever. And the fates had deemed them mine. I must have done something decent somewhere along the line to earn this. I'd walked away from one family whose terms for loving were not mine. I'd made the right call.

Karma. Perhaps she'd been named that for a reason.

Thank you for reading Papa Bear for Darius. Next in series is A Mate for Hudson.

Next in Series: A Mate for Hudson

Available here.

It all started with a crime...

Omega wolf shifter Hudson was set up—set up for a crime he never committed. Following the advice of his pack's seer, he fled in the middle of the night to find a new life in the desert. He finds a job at a greasy spoon diner, and it's not much, but it's better than where he left, even if he has to hide his true self—his wolf. When

Karma comes in and offers him a new job at a shifter night club, he jumps at the chance. As much as he loves his freedom, he misses being pack. A job isn't pack—but it might fill the void.

It all started with a blind date—a bad one.

Alpha bear shifter Shane is sick of dating; it always ends in rejection. His bear is longing for more than one-night stands—he wants a mate and cubs and all the things he knows he will never have, not once they find out he's latent. Omegas want strong alphas who can protect them with teeth and claws, not alphas stuck in their skin. But when his roommate sets him up on *one last date he begrudgingly agrees. How bad could it be? Getting punched in the face, a broken nose, and needing to be saved by an omega bad—that's how.*

So why is his bear crying out Mine?

A Mate for Hudson is a sweet with knotty heat M/M shifter mpreg romance served up with a side of daddy yums, an unexpected pregnancy, and a guaranteed HEA. It features a bear who can't shift, an omega embarrassed by his past, a found family, an adorable baby, and some familiar faces from the Omegas of Animals universe. Each book in this series can be read as a standalone. If you like your alphas hawt, your omegas strong, and your mpreg with heart, download today.

About the Authors

Lorelei M. Hart is the cowriting team of USA Today Bestselling Authors Kate Richards and Ever Coming as well as Ophelia Heart, another bestselling author. Friends for years, the trio decided to come together and write one of their favorite guilty pleasures: Mpreg. There is something that just does it for them about smexy men who love each other enough to start a family together in a world where they can do it the old-fashioned way.

Sign up for our Newsletter here.

Check out the Shifters of Distance

The Crimson Cliff Pack Series

Lorelei's Amazon Page

Printed in Great Britain
by Amazon

52450899R00083